BARB!
Thanks for the
Inspirations
DJR

MEN OF THE COMPASS

D.J. RUCKMAN

authorHOUSE®

AuthorHouse™
1663 Liberty Drive
Bloomington, IN 47403
www.authorhouse.com
Phone: 1-800-839-8640

© 2009 D.J.Ruckman. All rights reserved.

No part of this book may be reproduced, stored in a retrieval system, or transmitted by any means without the written permission of the author.

First published by AuthorHouse   12/9/2009

ISBN: 978-1-4490-4672-9 (e)
ISBN: 978-1-4490-4673-6 (sc)
ISBN: 978-1-4490-4674-3 (hc)

Library of Congress Control Number: 2009911732

Printed in the United States of America
Bloomington, Indiana

This book is printed on acid-free paper.

Dedicated to my son Cade
and my granddaughters Alexis and Caitlyn,

May your lives be as adventurous as mine and
may your inherited compass guide you home.

ACKNOWLEDGEMENT:

Many thanks to my Surveyor Grandfather who passed on to me a built in compass.

    Special thanks to Scott and Ann Waters and their daughter Mallery for their insight and editing suggestions; my surveyor brother Bill Cash and Beth and Michael, for their allowing me to be a part of their family; my Montana born, bigger than life brother, Jim Haworth; who always stays true and walks tall; my West Texas big heart brother Michael Horn, who always rises to top, helping others along the way; my Lady Shellie for her upbeat heart and my Mother Eloise for her undying devotion to her sons and daughters where she is unfailing.

PRELUDE

One of mankind's greatest discoveries was kept a secret for 1400 years. In 450 BC the Chinese discovered that a type of stone known today as Lodestone, after being struck by lightning became magnetically charged. Iron tools became stuck to it. When a small sliver of iron was rubbed with this magnetite ore and a piece was floated in water thru a straw or piece of cork it would orient itself in a north- south direction. The Norsemen, at about the same time, also discovered it. The compass was born. However, mysteriously, it was not discovered and used in English ships until around 1100 AD. Those few that knew of the Compass's magic qualities kept their secret and used it to their advantage to sail to destinations even when you couldn't see the sun or stars. Ancient Ireland was never completely conquered by the Norseman or Danes or many other invading tribes. Ireland remained a stronghold of different tribal colonies from 300 B.C. onward, exerting control over different parts of the island, always creating constant feuds between tribes, many of which were completely wiped out by various plagues brought by the next new invaders. The Irish were thusly a co-mingling of many different peoples. Norse and Danish raiders arrived in Ireland from 100 A.D. onward, and used it as a base to raid Roman Britain. In 367 A.D. the Irish Scots, Picts, Saxons and other sea raiders attacked and overwhelmed the Roman Britains. Weakened and in defeat, this started the decline of the Roman Empire in Britain. Legend has it that the Raiders would wait until foggy weather to raid; then paddle away into a dense fog to escape pursuit by the Roman British. Irish and Norse legends both describe voyages to a New Found Land across the ocean to the west. This was also kept a secret from the Roman British. The ancient order of Druids and their pagan way of life was swept away by Roman Christian Doctrine. The few remaining Druids sought sanctuary in wild Ireland. Using their ancient knowledge of the natural world they allied themselves with these wild Irish and Norse Peoples and sailed with them to new destinations and grand adventures bringing with them the Magic Compass.

CHAPTER ONE

RAIDERS

The Britons were gaining. The raid into Roman Britain had been a success until they ran into a flotilla of Roman warboats returning from Normandy. Looking out to the west Dante spotted the dense fog. "Turn into the mists. We can lose them there. Row faster, it is our only chance." The sea bound clouds came in silently as the warboats entered the thick soup. Lost in the sea mists is a sailor's worst nightmare. The men groaned; some said prayers to Odin and various other Gods of their tribes. All sailors feared not being able to see the stars or the sun or moon and the men at the oars were no different.

"Hold your tongues and keep rowing. If you don't wish to be a slave, keep on rowing. Wizard Dante can save us with his magic. Do not lose faith!" Eric shouted above the noise of the waves lapping the sides. He called to Dante," Can you keep us on course? If they catch us we will be destroyed."

"Aye, I checked our course as we came in. The magic needle has never failed me. If we row the opposite course as we came in we can keep going. I will keep you on course." Reaching into his robe he untangled the compass needle and dangled it from a woolen string. "I will man the rudder. Have the other boats stay close. We will keep rowing and outrun our pursuers." The men at the oars grumbled but kept up the pace. Hours went by and still they could not see farther than the boat behind them. The men were beginning to succumb to their fears. If they hit a hidden reef they would all be drowned.

Eric moved up next to Dante and whispered, keeping his voice low so the men wouldn't hear, "Dante, thou must slow down. The men are afraid. We have lost the Romans. They didn't follow us into the mists. We must slow the boats and rest the men."

"We are in no danger. I have navigated these waters countless times. If we keep going we will be home soon. I will calm the men." Dante raised his hands and began a chant, sending a spell of visions of beautiful skies and flat seas. The grumbling stopped and the men fell asleep where they sat. Sensing Dante's power, Eric sat down and put his head in his hands, hoping the skies would clear. Many times he had gone to sea with Dante and his Magic Compass Needle had always kept them from harm, but still it unnerved him. Closing his eyes he drifted off to sleep, lost in Dante's spell.

CHAPTER 2
CHANGES

A full moon had come and gone since Thadon had fled his father's castle. Having been on a hunting trip the few weeks before he was forced to flee, he had noticed a change in Thain upon his return. That evening he awoke about midnight with an ominous feeling. Being a bit hungry, he had been in the kitchen area when he overheard his older half brother and his brother's new healer discussing his father's demise. The healer's smooth voice drifted to Thadon, now cautiously hiding in a curtained nook.

"Your Father has passed on. No Healer could have saved him. You must banish or imprison Thadon if you wish to be the ruler here."

Thain was the oldest but not his father's favorite. Eric the Bold had made it no secret that he favored Thadon. As Thadon secretly listened in, the smooth voice kept filling Thain's mind with idea's of conquest, once he became the Overlord. Thadon had heard enough. He waited till they moved on. Silently, he slipped out of the castle. Darting in the shadows, he made his way to the stables. Donning his hooded woolen riding cloak and gathering up his long bow and an extra quiver of arrows along with the short sword he kept hidden there, he looked around at what ever else he could carry away with him. Moving through the stable he gathered another halter. A second horse would be an item he could sell or trade. Thain's stallion was tempting but might be hard to handle behind his own stallion. Selecting his fathers favorite mare Gida, who was due to give birth in a few months, would add to his holdings. Mounting his horse and leading a reluctant Gida, he rode all night and most of the next day, arriving in the evening just before a storm at his mother's family lands in Ossury, southwest of Eblana.

Now lying flat on his belly on the forest floor with a cool west wind blowing his long hair, he overlooked the trail to his father's castle and Eblana in the misty distance. The hillside sloped gently down this north face with an occasional rock outcrop jutting out of the thick heather. His mind wandered back to the words of aggression spoken against him by Thain and his new healer advisor. Who was this man with the smooth voice anyway? Where had he come from, and why was he prompting Thain to commit such an act against him? When he had told the story to his Mother she had been as mystified as he was about why Thain would suddenly turn against him. Her advice was to lay low for awhile, but he had plans and he was already tired of waiting to do the things which his dreams told him he should be doing. Thoughts of revenge and a new life now drifted through his mind as he and seventy two of his Irish cousins and members of the Corca-Laighde and Deisi tribes crouched in the wooded area south of his father's castle. Thadon had grown tall and broad shouldered. His Nordic grey-blue eyes were wide set with high prominent cheekbones. His chiseled chin framed by a long mustache and side handles gave him a lean appearance. Many hours spent in combat in the forests and villages had toughened him and sharpened his senses. His long blond hair with the center part pulled back into a war braid, fell nearly to his shoulders, hiding his somewhat overlarge and slightly pointed ears. The muscles in his jaw flexed as he chewed a dried strip of venison, pondering all that would take place this quiet evening. He felt the excitement that comes from night time raids. The rush a person gets with the anticipation of victory over ones enemies; hitting them before they knew you were there. Since his twelfth birthday he had accompanied his father and their Norse and Irish Raiders in attacks on the Roman-Britons. Those breathless escapes, running back to their hidden ships with woolen sacks full of plunder, had taught him how to slip in unnoticed, silent as ghosts, steal what they could, then slip silently away. Many times his survival was tested in confrontations and foot races with awakened soldiers. No hesitation, kill or be killed. Now, at age twenty, he was a seasoned veteran. Soon it would be dark, and the raid could begin. He glanced around at his childhood playmates and cousins, Brian, Shane, Shawn and Brandon. Being Irish, most of their time had been spent as farmers and sheep herders. They were young and eager for an adventure, hungry with thoughts of stolen treasures. They had all volunteered and recruited more men and boys than he thought possible. His plan was simple: raid at night while Thain and his followers were drunk from celebrating their recent raid into Britain. They would surely be asleep. The Roman British, having been weakened by plagues and constant raids, were still trying to recover and were not likely to respond to the raids from Ireland. He was still troubled by the change in Thain since this new healer had arrived and been advising him, but now was not the time for sentimental thinking; what was done was done. If it was war he wanted, so be it. He had convinced his cousins and their friends that they could steal gold, horses, stores of whiskey and whatever weapons they could find. He whispered to Shane, "Tell the others that we will split up after raiding the Castle stores and those that wish to go to sea with me can do so. They can meet me at the docks. Whatever they can carry is theirs to keep. Set fire to the barns and carry the straw to the castle and burn it if ye can." Shane was a few years younger than he. Still growing, he was not as tall as Thadon, but just as strong, and could run like the wind. Thadon admired Shane's fearless nature. Tonight's raid would test him, and Thadon hoped he would make it back home safe. He had promised his mother to look after him.

Shane asked, "What if we run into guards that are not asleep?"

"I cannot ask of you to kill a fellow Irishmen. I will act the part of a weary traveler. With my heavy cloak tossed over my head, I will capture the guards at the gates afore they can act. You and the boys can have at the stores and the barns. I will take Brian with me as he is the best with the sword and knife. Watch from here and I will signal when all is clear. Make no noise and we will catch them asleep. Stack as much straw as you can carry against the main gates and set fire to it. Shoot your flaming arrows over the walls to the rooftops. While they be battling the fires as they wake up, Brian and I will make to the docks and ready the boats we find. I will send Brandon, Shawn and several dozen others on ahead to the storehouses to rob them and ready the skiffs to carry us to me father's flagship. Make to the docks as fast as you can and load your bounties on the rowboats and meet me at the flagship. We will row away afore they know where we are. May the gods of war watch over you and keep you safe. Watch for me signal. Be like ghosts in the night. Spread the word, tell the others that we will honor them for their bravery this night and songs will be sung of our deeds."

Motioning for Brian to follow, Thadon raised his cloak over his head and stepped from the cover of the woods to approach the gates.

Walking as if drunk came easy to most Irishmen, and Thadon and Brian had no trouble stumbling up to the half asleep guards, mumbling that they had women to sell. The two guards were caught off balance and were quickly knocked unconscious. Thadon raised his long sword and signaled back to the waiting raiders. Silently, Brian and he slipped into the inner walls and descended to the storerooms below. They soon had their sacks full of all the loot they could carry. Grabbing a torch from a sconce on the wall, Thadon struck his flint and it quickly caught fire. Moving fast, they set fire to everything as they went. When they reached the west wall, Thadon threw a hemp rope over the window sill and tied it to a huge wood post. Descending to the ground, they ran as fast as their burdens would allow. The wooded hillsides leading to town and the docks were a welcome haven and they took a moment to catch their breaths. Looking back, Thadon motioned for Brian to look in the direction they had come. Flames were now shooting out of the Castle windows, turning his gaze towards the stables and barns, he saw one after another go up in flames. Soon the townspeople would awake and alarms would be sounded. He hoped that they would head for the castle instead of the docks, for it was the ships he was really after. If he could board and steal his father's flagship the Noria, he would fire arrows at the others and sink as many as he could.

"Brian," gasped Thadon, his chest heaving, "up ahead is ships master Dante's house. He is my father's and my friend. We need him to guide the boats; he is a healer and a master boatman. I know he will like our plan. I will wake him and try to get him to join us. You go ahead and meet with Brandon and Shawn and load as much as you can on the skiffs. I will meet you at the dock closest to the Noria."

Brian nodded and set of at a run. Thadon watched as his tall older cousin weaved his way through the trees. Brian was two years older than him and they shared many similar traits. His quick wit and warm personality hid the tough kid underneath. His father, now dead these last few years, had spent many hours teaching him the use of sword and knife. Being taller than most, broad shouldered and strong armed, he had won many a bout at the summer festivals. Watching him disappear into the night, Thadon gathered his sack and was soon at Dante's house. A few raps awoke him.

"Thadon, what are you doing here? If Thain finds you, he will imprison you."

"Yes, however, we have set fire to the Castle store rooms and stables and he will be busy battling the flames. I have come to ask that you come on a great adventure with me. I wish to go west with my father's boats and with as many men, women and children who wish to come along. I need you to guide us to Newfoundland where we will be free and start a new life. Bring your lady and son and as much as you can carry. Meet me at the dock to Noria. I have others already there and they await us."

Dante smiled, "So it is adventure that you seek and not revenge, a noble cause indeed. I too wish to be away from here. I will wake Sonia and Merlin and meet you there."

Brandon and Shawn had hid their two carts and horses in a dark alley a block west of the main storehouse. With Brian's and others' help they had indeed found the guards for the storehouses asleep and like cats in the night, they had knocked them unconscious. Brandon said, "Shawn, I will bring a horse and cart around to the doorway; load as many barrels of whiskey and weapons as we can carry. I will search for other goods and meet you here."

Panting from his efforts to carry the heavy wine barrel Shawn said, "We need blankets, clothes and any gold you can find; bring them and let us be off before more guards show up."

"Aye, said Brandon," I will get all that I can." With the other horses and carts soon full, they drove to the docks to meet Thadon.

True to his word Dante arrived with Sonia and their son Merlin. Thadon watched as they grabbed their bags. Dante was indeed a mysterious and imposing figure. Being taller than most and angular in body style with long flowing hair, gave him a not to be messed with look. His face was long and the robes he wore hid his thin frame. Sonia was tall and with her Nordic long blonde braids tied with red wool, she stood out. Grabbing her bags and helping Merlin out of the skiff she showed her dexterity. Merlin was young, maybe six or seven but was carrying a large sack of his own. Thadon hailed them, "Dante, can you call out to the ship and tell them you need to board to prepare the ship for a journey tomorrow?"

Dante, with his family in tow, boarded Thadon's boat. "Aye, but I'll wait till we are closer, row to the east side. When they awake they will be looking out to sea and not see the fires you have set." When they were in position Dante called out to the ship. "Men on board, prepare to be boarded, this is on orders from Thain." A young boatman looked over the railings and threw down a rope ladder. Dante and Thadon scaled the side of the ship and jumped on board. Thadon grabbed the young man from behind and wrestled him to the deck with his hand over the youth's mouth.

"Listen to me carefully and you may live to see the morrow. I am Thadon, and I take over this ship in my father's name. Will you pledge to me or do I throw you overboard? What say you? Nod if thou art willing to serve with me." The helpless man nodded and Thadon slowly released his grip.

"My name is John and I no longer have any loyalty to your brother. Tell me what thouest wish for me to say to prove to you that I served your father and Dante faithfully. With Dante with you, I will gladly be your man. Thain is different now. His men stole from my family and forced me into service. I have no love for traitors and murderers. Eric was good to me and my family. Since his death, my family has suffered greatly. I will gladly go with thou wherever it is thou goest. Anywhere is better than here."

"Well spoken," exclaimed Dante," I know this man and his words ring true to me."

"Rise and take my arm. I will treat you as a brother until you show me thou art not. Help us bring the rest of our people aboard. Hurry now; I will signal the others on shore to row as fast as they can.

"Aye," said John," place your cargo in the center of the boat, there is more room there."

Thadon could scarcely believe his luck. "Dante, see to the other boats coming in; they should be loaded with supplies. Get them all on board as fast as you can. My other cousins are to take the stolen horses with them and their loot to their families in Ossury. Those that wish to venture west with us will be at the harbor east of my mothers village. John, do you know who is on board my father's sister ship the Banth?"

"Nay," said John, "there are men there also, but I knowest not who is on duty. Since your father's death, Thain has recruited new men to man the boats. What do you wish me to do?"

"Come hither with me. Brian, Brandon and Shawn, you come too and we will try to board her and steal her, or burn her if we cannot have her. Dante, see to the readiness of Noria to get under way. If we are successful, I will signal you by bringing the Banth alongside." Brian, Brandon and Shawn and the others had finished unloading their stolen goods and Thadon and John jumped on board their rowboat for the short journey to where the Banth lay anchored. They drew up alongside the east side of the Banth and quickly scaled the hemp ropes to the deck. All was quiet; the crew was apparently asleep also. The three crewmen groggily awoke to see Thadon, John, Brian, Brandon and Shawn standing over them with short swords drawn. After a brief explanation all three agreed to swear fealty to Thadon. "Quickly now, man the oars and weigh anchor and prepare to bring her around," ordered Thadon.

Looking west towards the castle, Thadon could see horsemen headed down the hill running towards town. Thadon's men and the three new recruits soon had the oars dipping and pulling and were underway. In the dark with no moonlight it was difficult to see to shore as they were now half a league out and were pulling alongside the Noria. Thadon waved to Dante and he waved back. Thadon breathed a sigh of relief. For the moment he was out of reach of Thain, but knew that it would not take Thain long to figure out that the warships were no longer in the harbor. He hoped that all his fellow raiders had safely made off with what goods they could load on the horses. Sooner or later Thain would discover who was behind this night attack and try to seek revenge. Before leaving his mother's village, he had discussed with her and his family members his plans to go by boat to the legendary Newfoundland and start a new life. Now was the time to discuss this with Dante. "John, pull us along side the Noria, I wish to balance our crews and speak with Dante." barked Thadon like a seasoned ship's captain. Signaling the Noria, Thadon soon was aboard and took Dante to the rail to speak privately.

"Dante, you are the boat master. What do we need to do to the ships to ready them for such a long journey?"

Dante, fingering his mustache, answered, "Much needs to be done. To set out on the open sea we will need to construct boats with sails. Deeper hulls will have to be made. We need a safe harbor and many supplies if we are to venture west. Legend has it that St. Brendan, the Monk from Kilmalkedar, with a tall ship, ventured west across the open sea. He wrote stories of his journeys across the western sea. He described the lands he journeyed to. I have long believed these stories for they are similar to Norse legends. Many days and nights we will be at the mercy of the sea. We will need cabins built on board and rooms below for storage. Our Norse longboats are mainly manned with oars. We will need many timbers cut to raise the floors and rails. Do you have a safe harbor among your mother's peoples where we can do this?"

Thadon gripped the rails and thought for a moment on this before answering. "None that have the skilled shipwrights and tools that Eblana has." Then a bold plan began forming in his mind. "We must retake Eblana. Thain will gather several hundred Norsemen and some Irish slaves and march south to try and overtake us and punish my Mother's people and plunder and burn their farms. Thain will need weeks to outfit his army. Let us gather our people and double back and take Eblana while he is away."

Dante smiled, "Its no wonder that your Father favored you over Thain. You have a clever and devious mind. I think this will work. Many are already tired of Thain and his vengeful ways. Most will welcome your return. By the time he returns we can muster several hundred of your countrymen and those Norsemen who will be loyal to you and your father and defeat him. I like this. This will give us time to plan well for the trip across the sea. I have plans drawn for taller ships with sails and larger cargo holds with cabins for sleeping. I would welcome the chance to build such ships. We can trade for some fine Byzantine cloth for our sails. If we controlled Eblana we could do this. Your father and I discussed this very thing many times. It is a bold and daring plan; I like it."

They talked well into the wee hours of the morning; planning the timing and the scouting they would need of Thain's movements. Thadon asked," How is it that thou art the only one that knows the secrets of this thing thou call a compass; what magic is it?"

"Ah, that is a long story that stretches back many, many years with my ancestor the Druid Calcullen. It is time that I shared this story with you. Eric also was told this story and he kept my secret, lest it fall into enemy hands. In 336 Calcullen was escaping Christian Roman Britain and posed as a simple healer and herb man. He boarded a ship for Ireland headed for Eblana when a terrible storm blew them north and all seemed lost. Calcullen, however, had his lodestone compass hidden in his bags and convinced the captain that he needed to steer left if he was to reach land. Indeed he was right and soon they hit the shoreline and were saved. Calcullen kept his secret for many years as he traveled through Ireland eventually settling back at Tara to serve the high King as his healer. He passed his lodestone compass on to his eldest son who passed it on each generation and finally to me. My father's father was a blacksmith and made an iron needle, which when rubbed with the lodestone, passed on to the iron its magical qualities of always pointing in a north south direction when balanced in the middle from a woolen string. I still have the lodestone and several of my father's needles. Eric kept my secret and during long trips always took me along to guide him during dark stormy days and nights. It is this magic that we will use to sail west. I will pass on this knowledge to my son Merlin, whom I hope to be a great Sorcerer someday. We must keep this secret for it has always given us the advantage of guiding our warboats in dark weather, when are enemies art lost and confused. Will you keep my secret?"

"Aye, I am awed by your story. Thank you for believing in me and sharing this tale of things I have not heard of before now. It is the greatest story I have ever heard and we must not let Thain know of it as he will stop at nothing to obtain it once he knows you have left with me. I do swear to keep this knowledge safe and to vow to you on the word of my father who was saved by your magic. Let us sleep while we can. We have much to do once we reach the bay at Ossury and share our plans with my mother's people," said Thadon and he rolled over and fell fast asleep and had dreams of the battles to come.

CHAPTER 3
MIND CONTROL

Thain stormed through the doors to the inner chamber. The smell of damp wood still smoldering from the fires that the raiders had set assailed his nostrils and further inflamed his temper. "Craig," screamed Thain, "Where were the guards? Bring the gate guards to me, now." Craig nodded and motioned for his men to bring in the two guards from the front gate. He had anticipated that Thain would likely blame him and to avoid this he had to pin the blame on drunken guards. His men came in hauling the two guards who happened to both be Irish, which further inflamed Thain once he saw them.

"These two were on guard and were found knocked unconscious by the intruders, "announced Craig once the two were in front of Thain.

With long sword drawn Thain paced back and forth in front of the helpless men. "Tell me what happened. Quick now; speak up and tell me why I shouldn't lopp of yer heads. Who were these men and how did they get past ye?" The men looked at each other, both wishing for the other to speak. Seeing that his young friend was about to erupt into tears the elder of the two spoke up.

"It was midnight and we were at our post at the gate when two drunken travelers approached us and wanted to trade their women for any whiskey that we had. We told them to go away but they stumbled up to us as drunken men do. I pushed the first one away but then he pulled a club from his robe and smashed poor Oertel's head. I dodged their next blow, but they we on top of me and I too was knocked unconscious. I don't think they were drunk at all, jus pretenden like so's they could get close."

Thain continued to pace back and forth. "Did you see their faces, did you recognize them?"

"Aye, the one in front was your brother, Thadon. I didn't see the other's face before I was clubbed." Blood was still oozing from the sides of their heads, but hearing Thadon's name sent him into a screaming rage.

"Get them out of here, now. They disgust me with their pitiful story. Where is Malroc? Thadon must be tracked down for punishment. I am the ruler here and he will pay dearly for this. It is like him to come sneaking in the night instead of facing me like a man." He stopped pacing and turned to the doorway as a hooded figure made his way in.

"Malroc; it was Thadon who did this like a coward in the dark. The Irish bastard will pay for this. Craig; get me all the men thouest can find and we will hunt him down."

Malroc continued past Thain and with a whisk of his hands he sent a wave of energy at Thain that seemed to stun him. Stumbling, Thain staggered but managed to keep his feet. "Craig; what Thain really meant was for you to clean up this mess and bring us some wine and meat as he is hungry and needs to eat and plan for proper vengeance…..fools rush in…. there is no need to hurry. Come Thain, let us sit and plan like civilized men instead of madmen. Don't you agree, my young brash friend?" He motioned for Craig, who was still standing there stunned, "We will be in the main hall; remember, wine, food, and bring us a couple of young Irish gals for our pleasure. After all this fuss we need some entertainment."

Recovering, Thain nodded to Craig, "You heard him. We're hungry and thirsty. There is no need to rush out. We know where he is. Bring us some women. We will be in the hall." With swagger like a drunken man he turned and followed Malroc.

Stunned and speechless, Craig stood there momentarily dumbfounded. He shook his head then bellowed at his men. "You heard him. Be quick now. Get to the kitchen and bring some food. I will bring the women." Hurrying away, he wondered at what he had seen. Who was this Malroc? Where had he come from? How did he control Thain with just a flash of his hand? He must be a Druid or a Sorcerer. He had heard of such men before, but that was supposed to be legend, not real. All his short life he had dreamed of something special happening to him. He longed for power that comes from being with other men of power, and no one had come close to the realm of force he had felt when Malroc had waved his hand at Thain. Real power: not just physical brute force like him. He knew he was considered a bully. He had beaten all the men he had faced. Thain had brought him out of the jail that Eric had put him in and made him his man at arms. Women; so they wanted women. He liked the thought of lots of women to do with as he pleased. For years he had dreamed of days like this, where war was eminent. Adversity was all he had known since he was kidnapped by the Romans as a young boy and made into their slave. The forced labor had made him strong. He stole food; fought hard; survived and escaped when he was eighteen. Now he had power. Not as much as he wanted. He could barely remember the village he had been born in. He had escaped the Romans and the Norse Irish had become his family. He admired how they took what they wanted. Eric had become displeased with him for fighting with a local Irishman over another man's women. The man had died from his wounds and the villagers had demanded that Eric punish him. To please them and quell local riots he had been flogged and put in wooden locks. Recovering in a cell, he had learned that Eric had died and Thain had taken over. Tonight would be fun. Big deal that raiders had hit them hard and nearly burned them to a crisp. Malroc was right. Why rush out like mad men. There was plenty of time for vengeance. Have some women, eat and drink. Think of ways to strike back. Thadon was responsible for the attack and they knew where his family was from. Ossury: land of the Old Irish Clans. Legend had it that their warriors could change themselves into eight foot tall naked demons with just a gold cloth neck band and a sword and shield. They would rush screaming at their enemies and cut their way through. The Romans had quit trying to conquer them and had left them to their farms and villages. The Irish tribesmen were much too savage and wild for the organized formations of the Roman legions. Besides, they didn't have anything the Romans needed, so they left them alone. He wondered what Malroc had in mind as he tied his horse to the rail in front of O'Caollaidhe Tavern. Soon, he was on his way back to the castle with three young women in a buggy. They found Thain and Malroc in the main hall. Food and wine, fresh women, he liked that. He listened intently from his place behind the table hoping to hear what was being said.

"Thain, let us send some assassins to Ossury and catch Thadon off guard. He will expect us to amass a great force and go marching out after him. Let us do the opposite and lull him into believing he is safe for the moment. Get three or four of your best assassins and send them to Ossury to attack him while he is at his Mother's home. Offer them a large reward for his capture. Make it fifty gold Roman coins to the men to return with him. Meanwhile, you can make other plans and build more warships."

Thain smiled like a half drunk puppet. "Craig, send men to Ossury and capture Thadon. I will reward them with fifty gold Roman coins. If they fail, I will send you. Now go, be gone with you. I have wine to drink and women to please me."

CHAPTER 4
OSSORY KINGDOM

Saralynn, Thadon's mother, was at the docks at Ossury Bay when Thadon's ships came upriver. Her Irish people were used to war. They had known little else. Fighting for your life was an everyday existence. It's not that they liked war; it was that they accepted that war was always inevitable. Whether it was fighting over boundaries, or food or another man's possessions or his woman, it seemed it always led to war of some kind or another. So be it. Let's get it on. What do you want us to do? We are ready. She watched as Thadon and Dante disembarked from Eric's warship and gave final orders to their men as they approached her and the gathered members of the Corca Leighde and the Deisi Tribes.

"Greetings, Mother, this is Ships Master Dante; we have much to talk about. Dante, this is my mother, Saralynn, and my cousins." Dante bowed respectfully as if being introduced to a high Queen and awaited her acknowledgement before he arose.

Seeing this act of respectability, Saralynn blushed slightly and beckoned Dante to rise. "Please, arise Sir Dante, I know of you and your family's long history. Thou art welcome here in Ossury. My people art here to know what it is thouest wilt tell us."

Dante arose and glanced at Thadon. "It is your son, the young Prince Thadon that I serve and would ask that he tells all of ye that art gathered here of his bold plans." It was Thadon's turn to blush slightly and he took a moment to look into the eyes of those who had gathered at the docks this day. As his gaze fell amongst the gathered men and women, he was proud and afraid at the same time. These were the survivors of many wars and conflicts. He saw pride and determination in the eyes of these people who met his gaze with strength and fortitude reflected on their faces.

Breathing deeply he began. "We have dealt my Norse half brother a severe blow. Soon he will mount a large force and come here to punish me and my Mother's peoples for burning his stores and stealing his ill gotten goods. It is my intention to skirt his forces and backtrack to Eblana and retake her while he is away chasing ghosts. I would ask of thee this day to join me and fortify your holdings and bring all of your combined strengths together so that we defeat this evil inside him. He was always mean acting and bullish to me but never like this. He is different now and seeks power over us. Fight beside me and join the ancient Kingdoms of Ossury and Eblana together for the mutual benefit of all our peoples. I ask that if we win this war that I be allowed to stay in Eblana and build great ships for a journey across the great sea to the west and sail with those who will accompany me to Newfoundland. Once we land, as St. Brendan has written of, we will establish a trading colony greater than the world has ever known. It is my vision that all will prosper and that we can eventually defeat the Roman British and establish a lasting peace and prosperity for all."

A hush fell over the crowd as they took in all that he had said.

It was his mother who recovered and spoke first. "Thadon, you speak with great vision and you leave us breathless. Legends of our people tell us that one day a leader will come with a great vision that will free and liberate all that will follow him. My ears hear thou words. I believe that the legends are true and that you are this leader. As a chosen elder of my tribe I gladly join you in this battle and I pledge our family to fight to the death." She turned to the crowd, "What sayest thou? Ye have this day heard the voice of a great leader. Does thouest believe in his words as I do and wilt thou fight with me, for I have waited my whole life for a chance to strike back at the Invaders. I am ready. Art thou?"

With those few words she instilled in all that heard her, hope and dreams of a destiny that the legends had told of, and the crowd exploded with a fervor that had not been seen or felt in a hundred years of oppression. Thadon and Dante looked at each other with shock on their faces. Never had they thought that this dream would be so infectious that the people would so readily accept it as their destiny. Their fellow conspirators who had landed with them began chanting and dancing and further excited the crowd with their exploding spirit of joy at being so well received. It was like nothing that Thadon, Dante or Saralynn had ever experienced.

Ten days came and went and no word from the assassins. Thain was in a furious mood and had sent for Malroc. "Your plan has not worked; does thee have another plan? Thadon is still free, and I am growing weary of waiting for him to come to me as thouest foretold."

"Ah, my young friend, I can see that you are indeed ready for some action. Here is my plan. We will go drinking and raising hell at the taverns on the Wood Quay. We will let all the people see you and then we will start a brawl with some of the locals. We will fake that you have been knocked into the river and drowned. After a few days of searching for you, men will ride to Ossury with the news that you have drowned and that it is safe for Thadon to return. When he comes in you can ambush him and you will have your revenge. Until then you can find me in your Father's quarters studying his charts. I find it fascinating that he has crossed the seas in foul weather and found his way home. Do you know the source of the magic that guided them? Did he have a ships master who always went to sea with him?"

"Aye, his name is Dante. My father would not put to sea without him. He is also a healer of some sort. My Father would not travel the seas without him."

"What does this Dante look like?"

"Tall, thin, broad shouldered, long dark hair. He is not Irish. He always kept to himself. I think he left with Thadon. No one has seen him since the raid."

"What type of healer was he? Was he an herb man?"

"Aye, he was always passing out remedies for our ailments. They always worked. No one knew how he did it, but the men rowing the boats said that he had a magic way of always keeping them on course, even in storms and dark cloudy nights when they couldn't see the stars. The men would always be in a panic when they couldn't see the stars, but he never was. Why do you ask? Do you know this man?"

"Mayhap, mayhap I do. Are there any of his potions that I might study?"

"Aye, he gave me a potion for stomach cramps and I still have some left."

"Where is it? Bring it to me at once."

"Why the hurry, he is not here. We have other healers."

"Do as I say, for if he is who I think he is, he holds a key to great wealth. His real name is Calcullen and I have searched for him for many years. He has a magic metal called a compass. He who possesses this magic can cross the seas in any weather. The Romans would give a ship full of gold for this compass. "

Two weeks passed and Thadon had not received any word of an advancing army. Thadon took this time to spread word of the upcoming fight and the villages were full of new arrivals from Waterford, Cork, Kerry and Limerick. The dawn of the third week arrived with news that a mounted group of twelve men were headed their way from Eblana. Puzzled, Thadon, Dante and several dozen others rode out to meet them. They met on a hill a league north of the village. Thadon signaled a stop and called out to the oncoming riders who had also pulled up. "Men of Eblana, I see that you fly the colors of my father Eric. What message do you bring us?"

The eldest of the group, a man Thadon recognized as one of his father's former trusted named Creidon spoke first, "Hail Thadon. Thou brother Thain is no longer in Eblana. Their was a fight at the O'Caollaidhe Tavern on the Wood Quay three nights hence and a drunken brawl erupted, wherein Thain was knocked through a railing into the swollen Liffey River and was swept away. We searched for him for two days with no sign of him being found. We believe him to de drowned. Your father had told me of his plans to name you as his heir. Fighting and looting has been everywhere. Those with me today were loyal to your father. We came to ask thou to return and restore order. What sayest thou? Wilt thou return with us? Does thou havest men who will fight for you?"

Momentarily dazed by this unexpected turn of events, Thadon glanced at Dante who raised his left eyebrow and nodded for Thadon to answer. "Creidon, will you and your men ride with us to Ossury village, wherein we will form a plan and gather our men? How many men does thou thinkest it will take to put down this unrest and restore control," answered Thadon watching his eyes.?

"Aye, we welcome the chance to ride with you. Your raid three weeks ago showed us that thou art capable of leading men. I believe that others will join us once they see you returning. Can you bring several hundred of your kinsmen with us? With that many descending on Eblana with you, more will fall in line and stop the looting and infighting. The sooner we return the better our chances are of taking control," answered an anxious Creidon.

"Let us ride then to Ossury. I have men waiting to ride. We can soon leave with three hundred men or more. Tribesmen fighters are arriving daily as we were planning to return and wrest control from Thain. This news is well received. Thank you for this news; your support will be rewarded," spoke Thadon, like a man well beyond his one score years. With that he turned and spurred his horse at a fast gallop, for he could not wait a moment more to tell his mother and cousins this news.

CHAPTER 5
ENLIGHTENMENTS

Dante called Thadon to the door. "Walk with me outside where we will not be overheard." They left the crowded tavern and headed towards the docks. "What seems easy is never so. I have lived long enough to know that things are not always as they seem. Until we know for sure that Thain is indeed dead we must assume that he is still alive and maybe setting a trap to snare us into riding into Eblana unprepared."

Thadon, caught off guard by this possibility, stopped walking and turned to look directly at Dante. "Why do you suspect this? Are these men lying to us to deceive us?"

"Nay, nay, I do not believe so. I think they may be fooled also. These men were loyal to your father and not part of Thain's inner circle. I cannot detect any insincerity in their words. They believe what they have told us to be true. However, none of them were there when this fight took place and Thain's body was not found. He could still be alive and setting a trap. I believe we should wait a few more days or weeks and add more men to our force. I would like for us to split up. I will man the boats with one hundred men aboard the Noria and the Banth. We can let Brandon or Brian captain the Banth and I will be on the Noria. If indeed this is a trap, caution is our best offense. With the Irishmen arriving daily, you could have five hundred hungry villagers with you by weeks end. When you arrive in the hill country south of Eblana, send in men who should come in from the west instead of the south. Search out any traps before you enter town. I will land two leagues southeast of Eblana and send messengers to you of our position. I will also send men posed as travelers into town from the sea road to learn what I can. If the Town is quiet it is a trap. If the town is wild it will mean no one is in charge. I hope for the latter. That way if there is a trap, we can come at them from two sides and catch them in the middle. Either way, if Thain is dead, we can rout these looters as they will not be a combined force. If Thain is alive and lying in wait, we will have a better chance of defeating him this way. I suggest that we inform the others of these plans and wait a few more days and prepare for the worst. Thain can be very devious as you know, and I suspect someone is controlling him. Until we find out more about life in Eblana, I believe caution is our best approach."

Thadon had been listening intently and now seemed confused. "Why do you believe that this might be a trap?"

Dante sighed deeply and pulled Thadon over to a bench. They sat down and again Dante sighed deeply. "What I am about to tell you is a very, very long story. Only a few men I have shared this knowledge with. Your Father was one and he kept my secret. Will you swear on the lives of your unborn children to keep my secret safe with thou and thou only?"

"Yes, said Thadon, I wish to know all that I can."

"Good, I will take that as an affirmation of your trust. Remember when I told you of my ancestor Calcullen?"

"Aye, it is a story I liked and somehow filled me with deep feelings for you that I never understood before," smiled Thadon.

Dante nodded his approval and smiled back; then began his tale. "I didn't quite tell the truth. Calcullen was not my ancestor. He is me and I am Him." A look of disbelief came across Thadon's face.

"That cannot be; he- you- would be nearly two hundred years old."

"Aye," grinned Dante, "In fact I am older than that. As a Druid Master I was taught the Druid sleep by my Father nearly two hundred years ago. Every fifty years or so, I must move on so that no one gets suspicious. There are others like me, and I fear that one that has betrayed our ancient order has arrived and may be advising Thain. When your Father unexpectedly died, I suspected it then. For it is his style to turn men against men to achieve his chaos. His name then was Malroc. I don't know what name he may be using now. Long ago he turned against our order when the Elders would not make him one of them. He used his powers against them one by one and has assassinated dozens of our order. I am one of the elders he has sworn to kill. He cannot do it by himself; I am stronger than he. He does it by amassing a large force under a leader that he has induced under his control. If he is here, death and destruction will follow, and no one will be safe. I believe that he may be working for, or will sell information to, the Britains. They want the ability to cross the seas in any weather the way that the Norsemen with me have done. In short, he wants my compass. It is the most valuable tool there is. He does not understand its magic. I received it long ago from a Mongol trader east of the Germanic lands. He acquired it from a very ancient far eastern people called the Chinese. Malroc has desired it for a long time and I have kept it from him. Like me, he must move frequently to hide his identity. He loves misery and torment, as his power corrupts and past deeds torment him. I have learned that for every good man there is an evil man. It is the natural balance of things. Like summer grows things and winter kills. It is a sad fact, but it is the truth. Men are at their best when things are at their worst and at their worst when things are at their best. To turn men's hearts to do good deeds they must have common goals and a common enemy. You have inspired your fellow Irishmen with your heroics and actions. They now follow you because they have been oppressed and have a common enemy in Thain and the constant invaders of their lands. We can use this to our advantage, for they will fight hard and valiantly when they believe in a common cause. Many, many years ago in Italy, Malroc used a similar ploy to deceive certain family members into believing that a cousin who had committed a heinous crime of assassination was dead and that it was safe for them to return. I was there and failed to warn them that it might not be safe to return to their hometown. Upon their return, the cousin and his evil followers fell on them, and all were murdered. I do not wish for this to happen to you. I wish to help you build great boats and sail to this new land as I have things I wish to accomplish there. It is there that a great new nation will be born. I wish to be a part of it. So let us be cautious and arm your men with swords, shields, bows and as many arrows as they can make between then and now. The men we may face are all hardened warriors and may be being deceived with false promises of loot and glory. I tell you all of this for I wish to make an apprentice of you. You have the inner qualities that are needed. As our order has dwindled since the Romans sacked our ancestral home of Stonehenge, I have searched for likely candidates to replenish our ranks, but alas, I have not found any, except you and, I hope, my son Merlin."

"What makes you think I would be interested?" asked Thadon.

Dante smiled, "I am descended from an ancient race of long lived peoples. It is why I was chosen. From all indications I believe you, on your mother's side, are also descended from my race. Long ago several members of our race left the mainland for these islands. That is why I came here. I have been looking for you and any others that are descendants of my people. I can see it in you and your mother's eyes and the spirit that emanates from you. This is a lot to understand in a short period of time. I do not expect for you to agree now. I tell you this to prepare you for the dangers ahead. But for now, we must return to the feast that your Mother has prepared. Let us enjoy their excitement and dance and frolic with them. It may be our last time for awhile to have any fun and to spend time with our families."

"Aye, this is a lot to think about. I have many questions, but to be truthful, a certain long legged lass has caught my eye and I am eager to return," smiled Thadon who arose, and together they rejoined the several hundred who had gathered and were deeply immersed in the magic of the Irish music, whiskey, beer and dance. Thadon searched the crowd for the black haired, blue eyed beauty he had been introduced to earlier. Her smell was still in his senses and he wished he had been more graceful when they had met. Some of the boys were quite rowdy and they had grabbed Thadon from behind in a good natured way. Unfortunately, he had spilled his beer on her tunic and from the look on her face she was not too happy with him. Dante had come along and he had left with him. Thoughts of Dante's story and thoughts of her crisscrossed his mind and blurred his normal focus. Shaking his head to help clear his mind he again scanned the crowded gathering for her. Shannon caught his gaze and blushed as she realized that he was headed straight for her. As he approached, he again made her blush when he bowed slightly as if he were at his Father's court. She had hoped to see him again and when he took her hand and led her to a quiet spot under the trees she was thrilled but tried her best not to show it. Her mother had many times told her to play hard to get and to not let a boy know she was interested in him but now found that game hard to play. His eyes were blue like hers and he towered half a head above her and she felt her body tingling from his touch. She had dreamed of a prince such as Thadon. Now he was here, looking into her eyes. They both tried to speak at once and smiled at each other's clumsiness. He invited her to sit on a nearby bench and she nodded her agreement. "I truly am sorry for spoiling your clothes. Can I get you something to eat or drink?" Thadon grinned at her, all the while holding her hand.

"No, no, I have had plenty and I thank you for finding me. It is wonderful here and everyone is so excited. I have never been to a gathering where so many are singing and dancing!" exclaimed Shannon all the while staring deeply into his eyes, hoping to see if he felt as she.

"Nor have I seen such merriment. My cousins and the folk of this region have always been known for the gaiety of their song and dance, but they are truly feeling their mead this evening," beamed Thadon. "Come; let us walk along the river. I know of a quiet place where we can be alone." Thrilled at the chance to walk alone with him she nodded her agreement; his hand never leaving hers, he led her off.

Dante watched them as they left the security of the crowd and headed into the dark towards the river. Knowing that Thadon's enemies could be nearby hidden in the crowd he raised his cloak over his head and followed them from a distance. Using his Druid sight he connected with Thadon's mind and lightly established a link that would not disturb the young man's enjoyment of his new found interest but would let him know if trouble approached. After all these years he certainly did not wish to lose him now to an unseen assassin. Staying in the shadows, he followed the young couple who were oblivious to everything except the excitement of the moment. Extending his consciousness, he searched for any others of ill intent who may be following the couple. Broadening his search he detected an evilness lurking ahead. No, not one, but two or three and they were heading towards the unsuspecting couple now kissing passionately as the river flowed swiftly past, echoing their moans. Moving swiftly he slipped through the dark to intercept this evil. Using his heightened and trained senses he focused his energy and gathered strength from the natural world around him. Just as they were about to launch their attack upon the unsuspecting couple, he unleashed that energy at the creeping attackers and their clothes burst into flames. Screaming, they jumped up from their hiding place and thrashed their way through the thick and tangled riverbank brush, wherein they jumped in and were quickly swept away. Thadon had disentangled himself from Shannon and had placed himself between her and any others who may still be in hiding. Not stepping from the shadows Dante extended the touch between his and Thadon's mind and told him silently that all was now safe. No others were about. Thadon stared into the darkness towards where Dante was hiding and for the first time in his life he was aware as never before. Shannon pulled on his arm seeking an explanation but he ignored her and concentrated on this link between his mind and Dante's. Amazed and startled at the same time he realized that it was Dante who was there in the dark. Dante stepped forward, acting as if he had just arrived, smiling as he came towards them.

"Perhaps you should find a more secure place to be together." Embarrassed, with many questions on their faces, they accepted his offer and he led them back towards the crowded gathering.

The next morning Thadon was up early and eager to meet with Dante to get a further explanation of the foiled attack. Dante was up early also, and Thadon found him and Sonia and Merlin eating a breakfast with Saralynn and his new found love Shannon. "Good morn to all," said Thadon, smiling as he sat at the long table next to Shannon. "Did any of you sleep at all? What a night. I didn't think they would ever quit singing and dancing." Beaming a broad smile, Shannon poured him a goat's milk and offered a piece of the roasted pork with a fresh biscuit. Smiling back, Thadon could tell all were watching how the two young lovers were acting and he relished the attention. Sitting next to her made him feel good inside. Are these the feelings of a man and not just a silly boy? Interaction with other women had always left him hollow. The stirrings inside him when he was around her were more wholesome, somehow very comfortable. He took another bite and nodded to Dante who was helping Merlin to another slice of pork.

His Mother broke the silence. "Dante, pray tell good sir, do you believe that Thain is dead and is it safe for you two to return to Eblana?"

He looked eager to tell but changed the subject, "I believe our first order of business is to recover from such a grand gathering. It has been a long while since I have seen so many folk happy with life and each other. Take Shannon and Thadon for example. I thought they would never stop dancing. Thadon, I didn't know you were fond of the dance.

It was wonderful to watch you two together. Sonia and I need to take lessons from you two. Merlin was very impressed with the musicians, especially the drums. I have promised to acquire one for him. Music soothes the soul deep within. Combined with couples dancing it is truly magic. A powerful force of nature that if harnessed could surely conquer the world. Don't you agree Thadon?"

Caught off guard, Thadon glanced at Shannon, then his mother, and grinned as he swallowed a large bite of the pork. "Aye, I find that it is indeed an empowering force. I look forward to the next time we can celebrate as we did last night. Mother, thank you for making it happen. Shannon and I had one of the best times of our lives." With that he leaned over and kissed Shannon on the cheek. "Dante, can we walk and talk, I wish to know more of our plans so that we can share them with the others. I, for one, would like to spread this joy over the whole world. Come, let us draw maps and plan our return."

"Oh, no you don't, I haven't seen much of you and neither has Shannon. Your grand plans can wait awhile. I have other plans for you this morning. I wish to show you something of our family heritage. Shannon, get hold of him. Dante, you are welcome to accompany us. Sonia, will you come also. This won't take long and it is important that we do it now," insisted Saralynn. She arose and everyone followed with Shannon and Thadon locked arm in arm. She led them to the large stone fireplace in the great room of the family home. Taking an iron from the hearth she began prying at a stone in the side of the hearth. Soon Thadon could tell that the stone was coming loose and began helping her slide it to the side. As the stone was pulled away it exposed a small space behind it. Saralynn reached in and took out a rolled sheepskin. She led them back to the long table and unrolled the skin. Fascinated, the group stared in amazement at the different markings on the ancient skin. "This map was given to my grandmother from her grandmother and then to me. They told me to keep it stored here for they were afraid that if the men would see it that they would leave and never return. I am tired of keeping this secret. You said that you wished to build great ships and venture west. I believe that this map could aid you and show you where you are going. Thadon, this map was made by your ancestor who made this same trip and returned. Unfortunately, when our ancestor father returned we were at war with the Osraige-

Erainn tribe which we are now at peace and joined with. Most of the men were killed in a great battle including the ones who made this map. Our grandmothers then hid the map and it has remained here since. They believed it was bad luck but I do not."

Dante came over and unrolled the map further to reveal a name in the lower right corner. He recoiled as if hit in the face. Emotion showed that he recognized the name; Emolac. Everyone was looking at him. He sat down and stared at the name. Slowly he looked from one to the other before speaking. "This map was made by Emolac, he is my cousin. Emolac is the one I have been searching for. We are all family. This map solves a mystery that has kept me awake many a night. I have searched long and far for evidence of what happened to Emolac. Legend has it that he immigrated to Ireland years ago and then vanished. Thank you sister, Saralynn, I am in your debt. You are my family. I suspected this and had told Thadon such and this map now proves it."

A silence ensued as everyone stared at the marks on the map. Ireland and Wales and England showed on the right side with the channel clearly marked to the mainland and Normandy. A great space with marks as waves showed to the west and on the far left were the markings of a great coastline. To the north was an island called Iceland and then a frozen coastline marked Grenland. Dante knew that this map gave proof to the legends he had so long suspected were true.

Thadon raised his eyes from the map. "Dante; how far is it across the sea? Can you tell?"

Dante, with a grateful look upon his face, touched Saralynn's hand, "If I be allowed to study this map, I might be able to tell."

"Take it, it is yours. I have kept it long enough. If it helps, then I am proud to have saved it all this time until you have arrived to claim it. By what you say you are my cousin, and if, as you say, we are both of the family of Emolac, I would like to hear more of your travels and the rest of our family," answered Saralynn, whose eyes betrayed a deep satisfaction.

"I am indebted to you for having kept this map all these years and for showing it to us now. There is much to tell you. I would like to stay a few more days with you before we set out for Eblana," said Dante with a look of a great weight having been lifted off his shoulders and the excitement of a small boy reflected in his eyes.

"I would like that as well," said Thadon, looking at Shannon, who blushed a deep red and smiled back, before glancing at Saralynn whose smile showed her approval.

The next week was a blur for Thadon and Shannon. They spent every evening together while Dante tutored Thadon and Merlin during the day on the Druid histories and the power that came from focusing on the elements around you. After the incident with the foiled attack the night of the gathering, Thadon was ready to learn all he could. Dante included Merlin in these lessons and a bond soon forged between Thadon and Merlin, which pleased Dante. Finally he had two pupils that he could pass on his knowledge of the elements and how to control and use them. In the evenings Dante met with Saralynn to share their family stories.

Dante and Thadon had been sending men, two each day, disguised as traders to spy on Eblana and learn what they could of Thain. It had now been three weeks and none had yet to return, which caused Dante to believe that things were not as they had been led to believe. His suspicions were confirmed on the following morning when a badly injured Creidon was brought in by some of Saralynn's people. They had found him badly wounded and burned several leagues east of Ossury. They had bandaged him as best they could and brought him to Dante and Thadon. As Dante prepared salves to apply to his wounds, he told them that he and his men had been attacked on the west side of Eblana as they were riding in. A lone man whose face was hidden under a hood raised his hands and the grass around them and their clothes had burst into flames. Creidon had been in the rear. His horse had bolted and he had managed to dose the flames with his water flask that he had been drinking from when the attack came. Men on horseback had pursued him when a storm and hard rain had come up and he had sent his horse ahead and had hidden in a heavily wooded mountainous area. During the next three days he traveled only at night until he had been found by Saralynn's men.

"Dante," said Creidon," who was this man and how did he attack us in such a way? Was he a Druid Sorcerer? I thought they were just of legends and not real."

"Be calm while I tend to your wounds. It is possible that he is indeed a Druid. He must have sensed your true purpose and your ties to Thadon and I. It is my fault that you are wounded. I should have told you before you left that one such as he might be there. We will not make that mistake again. I commend you on your escape, for not many survive an attack such as you have described. Rest now and drink all the whiskey you wish. It will dull the pain. The salves that I have applied will also diminish the pain and start you healing. It will take a few days but you will recover to fight again if you choose. Come, Thadon, we must prepare our forces and give them the weapons they will need to help us defeat this Druid and take Eblana."

As they walked to the barns where Shane, Brandon, Brian and the others were camped, Thadon felt a determination swell within him. His lessons had taught him to read other's thoughts. A natural talent according to Dante and the first step in controlling one's opponents. He reveled in his developing skills and was anxious for continued lessons. The one of turning another's energy into spontaneous combustion was much more difficult. He had managed to cause a goats hair to smoke briefly. Dante had told him that he needed to focus not only on his subject but the air and other gases escaping from the ground around him. Fire cannot exist without air. Gases are always present around us, as they are formed under ground. Decayed and dead things such as leaves, sticks, grasses and the bodies of all once living things make these gases. Bringing the air and gases into the right mixture tighter around his opponent's body helped ignite the natural fire within each living thing. During the last week he had stayed awake late at night focusing on the air around him. He had almost caught himself on fire. Now, as they approached those that would fight with them, he wondered what he would say. How do you inspire men to fight beyond their normal abilities? What Creidon had described and from what he had seen and heard from Dante, he knew this would be no ordinary battle. It would take a lot of cunning and planning to outdo this Malroc and Thain, if he was indeed still alive. He wondered if his new abilities might allow him to sense and see the legendary wee peoples. They had many magic's and perhaps if he could but find them they might help. Maybe Dante knew how to find and talk with them. Later he would ask, but now they were near the waiting men and together they must find a way to battle their enemies. After greetings were shared Dante suggested that Thadon pick a dozen or so of his most trusted friends and that they talk privately. This was done and soon a war camp of those most trusted men gathered for drink and supper at the Eremon Tavern. Crowded in a back room they ate and drank and shared their thoughts of the way to retake Eblana. Many different plans were tossed around but soon it was apparent to all that Dante knew more than any of them and they gave way to his plan. He told them of this stranger who could wield fire and control another man's thoughts. Many didn't believe him but were soon hushed by Thadon who assured them that this was true.

Dante continued," This man is a Druid Sorcerer named Malroc. He has burned Creidon, who managed to escape by pouring his water flask over his clothes. He is the one who has turned Thain against Thadon. All must carry extra water and you must watch out for this hooded stranger who might approach you. In order for the fire to work Malroc will need to be close to you. The farther away from him the less his powers are. He will also try to confuse you by turning your minds against each other but would also need to be close to you to do this. Stay true to your friends and do not let doubt enter your minds. He can be defeated by large forces of men. He will stay back away from danger. With his mind control, he will induce others with false promises to do his bidding. If we are successful in overrunning their forces I will engage and defeat him. Many years ago we fought and he escaped while I was engaged in saving some men from his burning fire. I too am a Druid. He wishes to conquer me so that he can steal the secret magic of my compass which has eluded him. He will stop at nothing to acquire this magic. He cannot defeat me by himself but enslaves men's minds to do his bidding. I believe that Thain is still alive and being controlled by him. I believe that he was behind the murder of Eric, for that is his way to create dissention among men and turn sons against fathers, brothers against brothers. He fills their mind with greed and jealousy. He is evil. He cares for no one except himself, so beware and do not be fooled by his lies. If he gets the chance he will try to control your thoughts." Taking a deep breath and glancing at the attentive faces, Dante continued.

"Here is my plan. We will split our forces. Thadon has picked you for you are all loyal to him. Each of you will lead a group of fifty men or more and will come into Eblana from different directions to cause as much havoc as you can. You will attack at night as you did before.

When you run into the men and soldiers of Eblana call to them and convince them that Thadon is the rightful heir and that they should join you and they will be rewarded with much gold and their freedom. Thadon is both Irish and Norse and many will wish to join him. If they do not join you, defeat them if you can or lead them to our other forces and we will defeat them together. I will use my compass and take two hundred men and go far out to sea and come in from the north. On the seventh day Thadon will arrive on a hilltop south of Eblana with a small force of seventy five men with three hundred hidden behind him. He will draw Thain and this Malroc out into the open and then withdraw to his men in hiding. By then the rest of us will come in from behind them and encircle them. When they realize they are surrounded I will confront Malroc and defeat him. I will depart tomorrow evening and we will begin our assault ten nights from then. Look to the hills north of the Liffey River at midnight on the tenth night and I will light a large fire to signal you. Each of you, find a hilltop where you are and light a large fire to signal me in return. When we see fires on the hills north, south, east and west we are to begin to converge on the village and win over as many converts as you can. All are to head towards the south, where Thadon will come out on the next morning and try to draw Thain and Malroc out into the open. Think on what I have said, and we will meet again tomorrow." With that he stood, and motioning Thadon to follow, departed, leaving the rest to ponder on this plan.

CHAPTER 6
LESSONS

Long into the night, Dante taught Thadon more of the Druid histories and how to use the natural forces around them to alter or change the makeup of things. Herbs and their uses had always been of interest to Thadon, and he excelled in the memory of the many potions derived from them.

Finally, late that night, Thadon asked," Who are the wee folk of Irish legend? Do they exist, and can we see and talk with them? Will they help us with their magic? Can I learn the Druid sleep?"

"Whoa, slow down, one question at a time!" laughed Dante.

With the look of an innocent, eager, hungry teenage boy, Thadon put forth his first question, "Okay, will the Wee Folk help us defeat this Malroc and change Thain if he is alive? Thain was always mean, but he is different since this Malroc has gotten him under his control. Maybe if we drive Malroc away Thain will return to his old self."

"That would be wonderful if they would. However, the Wee Folk very seldom get involved with mortal human worries and disputes if it does not affect them directly. They are the custodians of the ether. The ether world exists between our world and the world of spirits. The reason that we cannot see them is that they move at a faster speed than we do. To them we are stuck in slow motion. In order for us to see them or talk with them they must anchor themselves to a tree or something physical like a stone wall. Then we can see and hear them. If the ether is in danger of being altered by us they will intervene and stop those of us from causing damage to their part of our world. They, for the most part, create the music, harmony and art between all living things. We draw near to them when we create music, poetry or great art. That is when we have a chance to see and communicate with them, for they stop and listen to the magic in our songs or art. When those of us chose to destroy things and foul the air they try to intervene and cause the trouble makers pain and agony by tormenting their minds and giving them bad dreams and causing them to lose sleep and shorten their lives to lessen the damage being done. It is a slow process, and much damage and death can still occur before the vile ones are finally vanquished and they torment us and them no more. The ones being tormented sometimes call this insanity in their minds the Cardodon, meaning demons in the head.

If you wish them to help you conquer the vile ones you can do this by inspiring others to great heights of endeavor. They will help you by filling your mind with thoughts of chivalry and gallantry, the things that songs, poems, paintings and sculptures try to depict. This is their gift to those of us that will let them into our hearts and souls. They inspire us to great statements in these forms. When you speak to your men tomorrow morning let them know of the gallantry and chivalry of their sacrifices. The Wee Folk will be there with you and their magic will flow through you. That is their help. The vile ones can only threaten and cause chaos in men's lives and that is why good eventually triumphs over evil. The sad part is that during that time of strife before good deeds eventually win out over bad; a lot of people suffer and die. They are the unfortunate ones that are the victims of the constant struggle between good and evil. When you inspire men to rise above their normal existence, you shorten the time of struggle, and fewer people suffer. All we can do is to try and shorten this time, and that is why we soon engage these men of evil in our present conflict. We save lives and try to restore the magic of a human life so that they can sing, dance and celebrate the joy of peaceful existence."

"The Druid Sleep is complicated and requires years of study. It has many facets. Thou are just now beginning your study of herbs and I can sense from your interest that you will one day master the Sleep. It begins with the right mixture of food, drink, rest, and work that keeps us in balance. One of the main ingredients is a frequent mixture of honey, various herbs, greens, oat grains and the fish from the sea. They restore the health of the blood that flows through your veins and organs. As a Druid apprentice thou must fully study the makeup of your body. We do that by dissecting dead bodies and trying to save those that are severally wounded. The knowledge that comes from these studies, especially the wounded, where we can watch the blood flow and the heart pump, teach us how the body works. The juices of the wild mountain berries and grapes clean and restore the parts of the body that keep us in good health. I have studied the body my whole life and do not understand all of its functions. We are fortunate to come from a race of long lived people. That gives us more time to study and learn. Our Druid Order devotes our studies to the natural world around us and how we can maintain ourselves in good health. We have books that contain the studies, potions and remedies of those that came before us. The greatest of which is the Tome. It was lost to us after Stonehenge fell and sacked by invaders. I have searched for it many years now. Malroc may have it. If it is he that is here now we may have a chance of retrieving it. I am pleased that you have asked these many questions. A curious mind is your greatest asset. If we are fortunate to overcome our present difficulties, I look forward to studying with you and teach you all that I know."

Thadon was stunned by this simple yet complex explanation. He understood for the first time what he should now do and why he needed to act quickly and inspire those that would listen to him to sacrifice themselves for the greater good of all. His mind whirled and spun with the enchantments of this knowledge. Finally he had reason to be a leader. Most men have no idea why they are born, why they die, or why they do or did what they did. Without this knowledge they are blind and simply act on instinct without really achieving their true potential. It was up to men of knowledge to lead them in the right direction so that they could be fulfilled and have a meaningful life. With this realization, a great relief came over him. For the first time in his life he was ready to lead and had an understanding of what he was really fighting for.

"Thank you for explaining this to me in a way that I can understand. You have given me great peace inside my mind and fortified me with the understandings of what I need to say tomorrow to those men that will listen and follow. I will never forget this and will teach it to all who will listen and hope that they have the ability to understand. I now believe it is a great truth of life and I am forever indebted to you for sharing this with me. I was struggling and you have given me a freedom that is a beautiful and wonderful knowledge. I will share it with all those that seek it!" exclaimed Thadon with a new light beaming from his eyes.

"You are welcome; it is part of your training. You cannot move to the next level without first understanding these principles. When you are ready, more questions will come, for an inquisitive and open mind is your greatest asset and one you must constantly grow and nurture." Smiled Dante. "Let us get some sleep. Tomorrow we must go our separate ways and do our part in the great battle to come. Clear your mind and be at peace. I go now to be with Sonia and Merlin for it may be a long while before I see them again. Go to Shannon and hold her tight and fortify yourself with her love. You will need it in the coming days." With that Dante hugged him and left him to go to find Sonia, and the brief peace that comes with being with those we are fortunate enough to share love with.

Thadon's horse was lathered as he pulled up at the quaint cottage. Hearing the approaching hoof beats Shannon was joyous and leapt into his arms. They sat on the front porch and talked for hours until Shannon's mother bade them come in. She insisted that Thadon sleep in the barn since it was late. The next morning Thadon was up early and had a breakfast of eggs and ham that Shannon prepared for him. He kissed her longingly goodbye and waved as he mounted his horse to begin one of the most important days of his life.

There were already several hundred men and boys gathered at his mother's barnyard when he arrived. Dante was there and gave him a knowing nod as he rode in.

Shane sauntered over, "Did thou get any sleep at all last night and did thou kiss her good-bye for me and the boys too?" With that everyone laughed and slapped Thadon on the back as he walked to the barn to climb up on the wagon so that all could see him.

In as loud a voice as he could muster he proclaimed, "Aye, 'tis our women and family that we fight for, and I love her dearly. It is my hope that we soon return, for I intend to marry her when we take Eblana and unite the clans. All of you have suffered and been oppressed by those who would conquer us and steal our land. Today we march to fight for our freedom. We can rid ourselves of these evil men who would enslave us and steal our women. Ireland is mine and yours, and when we win this battle, it will send a message to all that hear of our bravery and strength that we will not be owned by anyone. Let us unite the clans and strike fear into their hearts for we are a people who this day vow to each other to fight as the screaming wild Irish that we are. Prepare yourself and grow stronger and taller as only the fighting Irish can do. Let the demon inside you out. When we run screaming at them and wield our swords as the wild free men that we are, we will strike fear in their hearts. Our children will write songs of our gallantry and bravery. Let it begin." With that he raised his sword over his head and screamed as an avenging eagle. The gathered men and boys screamed in return and so it began.

CHAPTER 7

HOSTAGE PLANS

Thain had been drinking all day. His foul mood darkened as Malroc found him slouched in a chair. "Your plan hasn't worked. Thadon hasn't returned as you said he would, and I grow weary of this place. None of the assassins have returned. I will send Craig. He will capture him for me."

"Craig will do. Send some Irish with him. They know the way in and out of Ossury. We'll have him capture a family member if he can't get to Thadon. Send writing materials with him. Have him leave a note that we will trade the family member for the compass."

"Aye, the Irish know the way, but we can't trust them."

"Capture their families and hold them hostage till they return. Promise them gold and the return of their families if they bring us Thadon or a family member we can trade. When Craig has them together have him bring me two of the thieves from your dungeon and I will make them aware of what will happen to their families if they fail us." With that he spun around and left Thain to his crock of whiskey.

The next morning Thain sent for Malroc. Craig had five men with him and two prisoners with their hands tied when Malroc entered the room. With a wave of his hand Malroc motioned for Craig and the other five to move back. "Prisoners, you have been found guilty of stealing from Master Thain." Malroc waved his hands over his head and then dropped them directly towards the prisoners. An invisible force slammed into them and they screamed and stumbled back falling to their knees. As they hit the floor their clothes burst into flames. Craig had never seen such and caught his breath as the dying men jumped up and tried to run, further enflaming the fire that consumed them. They fell writhing in agony, screaming as they died. Malroc turned to Craig and the five transcripts with him. "Bring me Thadon or one of his family members. You have just seen what will happen if you fail."

Three days later Dante and the two warships with one hundred men were well on their way. They rowed far out from land so as not to be discovered. In two days they would be north of Eblana and make land fall where they were not expected. Riding the swelling sea at night when the stars were not out always frightened the men. Dante dangled his compass and kept them on their course. On land and leagues away to the west, Thadon had split his forces into three bands of fifty men, keeping one hundred with him heading straight at Eblana. The others were to circle northwest and northeast and come into Eblana from the west, east and northwest. On the morning of the fourth day riders were seen coming hard towards Thadon's' men from Ossury. Runners hailed Thadon and told him of the approaching horsemen. Thadon mounted his horse and with his guard rode to meet these riders. As they approached Thadon saw that at the front of eight men was his mother who rode straight to him and dismounted. She grabbed his hand and led him to a group of trees where they could talk privately.

"What is wrong Mother? Why have you been crying? I can see it in your eyes." Saralynn could see the concern on his face. "Tell me, please. "

"Oh Thadon, Shannon has been kidnapped, and her parents were tied up. Men came in the night and attacked them while they slept."

"Shannon. Shannon. Why Shannon? This can't be! It just can't be. Which way did they go? I must go after them," exclaimed Thadon his eyes filling with tears then hardening in anger. "I will gather some men and track them and kill them all. Tell me, which way did they go? Did you find their tracks?"

"Yes, maybe five or six men. They were on horseback and headed this way. I gathered these men from the village and we tracked them until we lost their trail about five leagues southwest of here. I believe they are going around you and headed for Eblana." Saralynn held him and looked into his eyes. She knew it was Thadon they were really after and would try and use Shannon to trap him. The look in her eyes showed her fear for him. Fear that he may do something rash and fall into Thain's trap. "They're using her to get to you. You must take a deep breath and think this thing through."

"Damm them: Damm them all. I will make them pay for this."

Men of the Compass

"Aye, Aye, but let us plan, not just react. We will find these men and rescue her."

"When you lost them, did they go north or west?"

"We don't know. They split up and crisscrossed their paths and then we lost them in the forest. I decided to ride as fast as I could here to warn you, for I believe they did this to distract you and divert you from attacking Eblana. They left a note." With that she pulled a piece of cloth from her garment and handed it to him. On the cloth he read these words: "We will trade her for the compass. Bring it with you under a white flag of truce to the hilltop one league southwest of Eblana. If you do not, you will never see her again. Be there in seven days when the moon is full."

"I don't have this compass. Dante put to sea with it and we are not to meet for seven more days. I cannot do this. We must track these men and intercept them and take her from them. I must go now. Show me where you lost their trail," shouted Thadon.

"Aye, this is madness. I don't know which way they went. They could be anywhere. There are dozens of trails. I left two men to search for some trace of which way they went, but it could be days before we receive any information. There has to be another way. What is this compass anyway, and why do they want it badly enough to do this? Please tell me what is this thing? Why is it so important?" exhorted Saralynn, holding his hands and staring intently into his eyes.

"It doesn't matter, we don't have it anyway. It's a long story about a piece of magic metal that when dangled from a string at its mid point will always point north and south. Dante uses it to guide ships on the sea when you can't see the stars or the sun. He has had it for a long time and has kept it a secret. Dante believes that an evil rouge Druid named Malroc is the one who is seeking the compass as he has sought it for a very long time and will stop at nothing to obtain it." Thadon sighed and put his head in his hands and sat down on a fallen log.

"A piece of magic metal; a Druid; what else is there to this story that you haven't told me? " exclaimed Saralynn, raising her hands in frustration as she sat down on the log.

"Dante is a Druid Master and has been training me to become a Druid. Dante believes that Thain is not dead but is under the mind control of Malroc. He believes he influenced Thain to allow him to treat father, then let him die or poisoned him. He believes that Malroc had Thain fake his death to draw us back to Eblana unawares of an ambush. Now he has Shannon. He is a diabolical monster, and when I see him I will burn him to the ground." With that he concentrated on the fallen dry logs nearby and so intense was his anger and concentration that they began smoldering and the grass around them burst into flame.

Astonished, Saralynn jumped up and looked back at Thadon. "How; how did you do that? What else can you do? Why haven't you told me of this?"

"Dante has taught me to read a person's mind by his actions and the way he speaks and carries himself. He says that I am a natural mind reader and leader of men. I have been studying herbs and their healing powers and this power of fire. He has also taught me of the Wee Folk and how to use their magic to shorten the misery of the victims of evil men. Dante has taught me that reading your opponent's mind is the first step in controlling him and defeating him. As we have been talking I can see that Malroc is a desperate man and is trying to control me by making me react by impulse rather than being in control. He is thinking that I will rush out and fall into his trap. I must think like Dante and decide what he would do."

"Well, what would he do?" asked Saralynn, reseating herself next to him.

"Well, I think he would try to fool him and set a trap. All I need to do is act like I have the compass and be there to meet him. We could surround him with our men and try to force him into surrendering Shannon and spare his life for hers. If I can delay him long enough for Dante to arrive then Dante and our forces can confront him. But for now, let us send out a message to him that we will meet him seven days from now and deliver the compass. That will give us time to regroup with Dante. I will send groups of our men in different directions and wait along the trails that we know of and maybe intercept these men who have Shannon. They will be traveling slowly so as not to attract our attention and probably traveling at night. You rode straight here. Maybe they are still behind us. Come, let us form men into bands who will camp out along the possible routes that they might take and look for signs of their passing's."

With that they returned to the waiting throng of men and asked for volunteers to band together and search for this group of kidnappers and Shannon. "Who among you are the best trackers? I need volunteers to scour the trails leading from Ossury to Eblana to find the men who have kidnapped Shannon and kill them and rescue her if you can. I need five bands of six men each with a couple of good trackers in each band to find these trails and catch them if you can before they reach Eblana. My Mother and her men, as you know by now, lost their trail about five leagues south of here. She has told me that they are trying to get around us and reach Eblana. If we fan out and get ahead of them we might foil their plans. You have pledged your service and loyalty to me. I will forever be grateful to the group that finds her and rescues her. The outcome of this battle could be won if we rescue her before they get her to Eblana. They are trying to use her to get me to change our plans. We must not let this happen, but I cannot bear the thought of losing her."

With that said, dozens of men stepped forward and in a flash he had the five groups of men on horseback galloping off in different directions. Saralynn and Thadon watched as the last of the groups left the camp.

"You have become very wise, my son. Come, sit with me, for I need to tell you a story of your grandmother, my ma, who was also kidnapped and lived to escape her captors. The story will give you hope."

"Yes, but I need to send runners to Eblana to deliver our message. Please tell me her story as we ride, for now I need a piece of charcoal to answer their demands." Saralynn had anticipated this and brought along writing pens of charcoal. "Mother; please write that I will bring the compass to the hilltop southwest of Eblana seven days from now. Answer him not to harm her or I will seek revenge and destroy him. Write that if he gives her up unharmed in exchange for the compass, I will let him live and go free."

"How can you say this? You don't have the compass?"

"Aye, but he doesn't know this and by that time Dante will have arrived and he and I will confront Malroc and destroy him."

"Are you sure this will work?"

"Yes, send for Brian."

Soon Brian arrived and Thadon told him of his plans. "Go at night and when you get within bowshot of my Fathers castle shoot an arrow into the gate with this cloth attached. It will buy us time." Brian accepted the cloth and set out on a fast horse towards Eblana. "Mother, I must go in search of Shannon. I will put Shane in charge of Dante's plan. When you lost their trail were they headed northeast into the Eraini Mountains or northwest around them?"

"I believe that they were turning into the mountains for it would be easier to lose us on the forested slopes."

"I will take eight men with me and head for Galwinns Pass. It is there that I believe Shannon's captors will try and slip past us. It is heavily forested and it is there I will lie in wait."

"I will go with you," smiled Saralynn, taking his hands in hers and staring deeply into his eyes. What she saw made her both proud and sad that he must bear this burden.

"Thank you, Mother, for calming me, and making me see clearly what to do. I do need you by my side. I have sent for Shane. I will tell him of our plans and will meet you soon. Together we will rescue Shannon. Meet me at the north end with some supplies. We will begin our search. Shane accepted the charge of the men and Dante's plan. "Remember, if I am not back by then, watch for the fires on the hills north, west and east of Eblana. That is Dante's signal to attack. The next morning advance, with but 75 men, and then retreat once Thain and Malroc attack you thinking that you only have these 75 men. Retreat to the men that you have in waiting over the hill. Dante and I and the others will come in behind them and encircle them and destroy them. Be on the lookout for Shannon. If I haven't rescued her by then, try and find her and save her if you can. You are strong and brave. We will win, and soon we will take Eblana and build those ships we have dreamed of. I have asked the Wee Folk to watch over you and lend you their magic. I go now and will meet you soon. "Turning, Thadon mounted his horse and with Brandon and Saralynn they led their small band towards Galwinns Pass.

CHAPTER 8
MOVING TO BATTLE

The fog was so thick that Dante could barely see the Banth. He had guided them through with the compass and soon they came out of the swirling mists. He signaled the Banth across the choppy water that soon they would turn into the setting sun and make landfall. As they neared shore Dante searched for a deep secluded bay where they could hide the warboats for a few days. His plan was to leave Creidon and the seaman John with a fifteen men to man the boats and bring them to Eblana at the docks south of the Liffey River in two days. By then he hoped to have met up with Thadon and conquered Thain and Malroc. Waving back to the men on the boats Dante and his one hundred men set out on foot to march the three leagues to the hills north of Eblana.

  Galwinns Pass was a narrows of the ridge trails descending from the Eraini Mountains five leagues southeast of Eblana where the mountainous terrain changed to foothills. The moonlight shone brightly and a stiff cool breeze ruffled their hair as Thadon and Saralynn and their men lay in wait, watching for any signs of movement. The forest thinned out here into a natural bowl where Elk and Deer came out in the evening to drink at the numerous springs that flowed from the deep forest. Thadon had placed himself and most of his men on a trail that was above the natural bowl well hidden in Fir trees. He had placed Brandon fifty feet higher above them on a bluff that overlooked the trail crossing the open bowl. The sun was setting and the fall winds had come up and it was getting colder. Sitting still was causing chills to run over his body. He looked over at his Mother and she too was shaking. Moving closer he wrapped his woolen cloak around her and together they waited and watched.

  Glancing up at Brandon he sat up straight and forgot his chills. Brandon was motioning for him to look to his left through the firs and not across the opening. Looking through the quivering branches he could see the legs of horses slowly coming his way. They were not going through the open area but were skirting it on the very trail he was on. They were slowly heading his way. His men were further north on the same trail and he dare not call out to them. Picking up a small stick he threw it about fifty feet to the closet man. Donals looked up as the stick hit the ground near him. Thadon motioned with his thumb over his shoulder and put his index finger to his mouth for Donals to be quite, hoping that he would signal the others to be ready. Donals understood and sent the signal ahead. As the horses and men were coming directly towards him through the thick firs, he slowly stood up and drew his sword, motioning his Mother to be ready. Looking through the waving tree limbs, his heart raced and the shakes from the cold and inactivity grew till his teeth chattered and he shook all over. Darkness was descending as the lead horseman guided his horse around Thadon's and Saralynn's fir tree. Thadon sprang and grabbed the unsuspecting man from his horse and knocked him to the ground, hitting him with the butt end of his sword he knocked him unconscious. The man's horse panicked but Saralynn grabbed the reins and held tight. The second horseman wheeled his mount around and yelled ambush just as Brandon's arrow caught him in the shoulder and toppled him from his horse. Thadon ran straight at the remaining riders when he caught sight of Shannon with her hands and legs tied and her mouth gagged on a horse being led by the third rider. He placed himself onto the path of the charging horse and threw up his hands, causing the horse to jump sideways and rear. The rider pulled hard on the reins and turned the horse into Thadon, knocking him sideways into the thick branches of a fir tree. Before he could disentangle himself from the tree the rider managed to spur his horse and pulling hard on the rope leading Shannon's horse, he broke free of the trail and plunged downhill into the open area. He was soon galloping away.

 Jumping up, Thadon ran to where his Mother was holding the reins of the first horse. Swinging himself up, he was soon in pursuit. Kicking his mount hard in the flanks, he plunged downhill after the fleeing horses and screamed to his men," mount your horses; it's Shannon. Don't let them get away!" The escaping horseman with Shannon in tow galloped away. Thadon soon realized that his stolen mount was no match for the horses ahead. Anger and fire boiled inside him for not grabbing his horse as he looked over his shoulder and saw, in the now darkening sky, other riders coming his way. Were they his men or more of the kidnappers, he couldn't tell. Kicking his horse even harder didn't seem to have much effect on the lame beast he had chanced to grab. They were getting farther ahead. Realizing that the horsemen behind him would soon catch him, he pulled his sword and turned to meet the oncoming riders. He could see a dozen or so horses a few hundred feet apart galloping hard at him. The first horseman with his sword raised to strike swung his horse wide right then veered directly at Thadon to cut him down. Seeing this, Thadon turned his horse directly at his adversary. Then as they neared he cut to the right of the oncoming horseman giving him a frontal thrust with his long sword as his enemy swung wide to try and cut him. Thadon's sword struck first and caught the right shoulder of the astonished attacker, knocking him off his horse to the ground with Thadon's sword stuck in his right shoulder just above the armpit. Thadon swung his near- lame horse around just in time to see another kidnapper swing his horse wide to gallop off after the fast fleeing Shannon and her captor. Turning to the man on the ground, Thadon jumped off his horse and drew his belt knife as he approached the writhing man pulling Thadon's sword from his shoulder and trying to stand. "Do not move. I do not wish to kill you. Kneel before me and I will spare your life."

Seeing that the other kidnappers had abandoned him, the man fell to his knees and threw down Thadon's sword. "I yield and I recognize you Thadon, son of Eric. If you spare my life I will help you get your lady back if you will help me get my family from the Sorcerer Malroc. He forced us to capture Shannon by imprisoning our families. If we brought her to him he would set our families free. Now you are here and I am vanquished. Do what you will with me, but I know where he is heading and will hold her. Please tell me you will defeat him and know this, though I have done a terrible thing, I did it to save my family. "

"Where, where is he to hold her and how many men are with him? Is Thain under his control? Be quick man, tell me and I will do what I can to save your family."

"Yes, he has some power over Thain that we don't understand. Thain does what this Sorcerer wants. He ordered us to help him get the magic compass from you and Dante by us capturing your Shannon so he could force you to trade. If we didn't our families would be killed. To show us his power he burnt two men alive by waving his hands at them. They screamed and died a horrible death. Kill me if you will for I have done a terrible thing, but we had no choice."

Just then Brandon, Saralynn with Thadon's horse in tow, and his other men pulled up. Thadon yelled." I'm okay. Chase after them. Run them to the ground. I will be right behind you after I question this man. Mother stay with me, for this man needs your help." With that Brandon nodded and then spurred his horse hard and he and the others galloped off after the fleeing kidnappers.

"Be quick now; where are they headed, and how many men does he have? Tell me all that you know and I will bandage you and leave you a horse. You must promise to fight on my side of this battle and to never be my enemy again." Tears came to the man's eyes and he sobbed his thanks, "Shannon was to be held at O'Caollaidhe Tavern on the Wood Quay until the Sorcerer arrived there in two days. I don't know how many men he has but all are afraid of him and Thain's men do his bidding. Please save my family; my name is O'Toole. I have a wife and three small children. He has them in Thain's cellblock in the castle."

"I will do what I can. If you make it to Eblana, tell all that I am coming. Recruit as many men as you can to help me and I will forgive you." Having tied a cloth bandage around the man's shoulder in a sling fashion, Thadon and Saralynn stood and handed the reins of the slow horse Thadon had been riding to O'Toole. Darkness had come and a cold wind blew in their faces as they galloped their horses after the others. With no moon out and rain clouds coming in, they knew that their chances of catching the fleeing riders this night would be slim. The trail wound around a wooded hillock and they soon came upon a small farmhouse. Standing next to the farmer and his wife and kids were Thadon's men holding their horse's reins while the horses hungrily grazed on the lush heather.

Brandon waved to them, "We lost them. These farmers have seen no one come this way. They must have doubled back in the forest. Mayhap we could light torches and backtrack and pick up their trail. Looks like a bad storm coming in. It will be a cold rainy night. What thinkest thou? They can't be far off and soon they too will need to seek shelter."

Nodding to Brandon, Thadon turned to the family. "My name is Thadon, Son of Eric. This is my mother, Saralynn of Ossury. We track several evil men who have kidnapped my Lady Shannon and we need your help. Thou knowest this area. Are there other farmhouses or barns nearby where they could seek shelter from a storm?"

Over the rising noise of the oncoming howling wind the farmer wrapped his coat around a small boy he held, "I am Conner and I lend what help I can. My cousins and I have farmed here for many generations before your father conquered Eblana. He treated us fairly and we are sad that he is gone. There are four other farmhouses with barns within a league of here. This cold wind and rain coming in will not be fit for man nor beast to be without shelter. I don't know which way these people were headed, so it is hard to say where in this black night they might be. You be welcome to spend the night in our barn. Your Mother may stay with us in our humble cottage. We have a spare small room with a comfortable bed where she will be warm and dry."

"Thank you for your kindness. Mother, stay with them and I will return soon. The wounded man we left behind will stand no chance in this cold rain. It is a while before the storm sets in. Brandon, help me fetch this man O'Toole as I would question him further as to things in Eblana. The horse I left him with is near lame and without our help he might not make it through the night. We will return soon and join the men in the barn." With that he and Brandon mounted their horses and rode back the way that they had come. Soon they came upon the struggling O'Toole slouched across the neck of the horse Thadon had left him. The winds were now much colder and the rain had started falling, filling the evening sky with ominous forebodings of worse things to come. Reaching O'Toole, Thadon grabbed the reins and called to him above the wailing wind, "Hang on, there is a farmhouse and barn up ahead. We will take you there."

Raising his head O'Toole moaned, "The others I was with. They were here. Your Lady Shannon is still with them. Since I couldn't ride fast they left me and headed off north towards that yonder hilltop and the safety of the forest. They wanted to get as far away from you as they could before this storm sets in. They told me to fend for myself. They were going on to save their families."

Thadon glanced at Brandon who nodded and smiled, "Let's follow them, with this wind howling they won't here us coming. O'Toole, can you make it? A cottage is up ahead a half a league."

O'Toole nodded and smiled faintly. "I told them what you had said but they are still afraid for their families, held like mine by the Sorcerer. They are more afraid of him than you." Thadon reached over and tightened up the sling bandage around O'Toole's neck.

"Tell the others that we have gone after Shannon. Tell them which way we went so that they may follow after the storm. Will ye do that for me?"

"Gladly, you have given me hope for my family. I will do all I can for you." With that Thadon and Brandon set off in search of the trail left by the fast moving horses in the now damp soil. The howling wind had slowed but the rain continued and both men wrapped their woolen cloaks tightly around themselves. After traveling a short distance back down the trail that O'Toole had come from they found the tracks crossing to the northwest. They followed at a slow trot as the prints led along a well used trail that indicated that one of the Cottages may lie ahead. Soon they came upon a clearing with the outline of a barn and further along the trail a cottage with smoke rising through the rain from its fireplace. Nodding to Brandon, Thadon guided his mount past the dripping trees towards the sheltered side of the barn. Dismounting, they drew their swords and angled along the barn wall to a doorway. Slowly unlatching the wooden slide they slipped in to stand against the inside wall till their eyes adjusted to the darkness of the welcome dry interior. Standing still and listening intently they could hear the horses in the nearby stalls moving nervously. Thadon's heart raced wildly at the thought that Shannon must surely be nearby. Kneeling now, Thadon motioned for Brandon to go right and he would go left.

A sleepy voice called out, "Who's there? Is that you Conner?"

Thinking quickly Thadon answered. "Aye; go back to sleep, all is well." Silently he moved towards the voice and soon came upon two forms huddled in the straw in a vacant stall. Sticking his sword against the foremost form he prodded the man awake. "Mister Conner, what, what do ye want? "

"I am not Conner. Move and you die. I am Thadon and you have wronged me and my family. Shannon, where is Shannon? Tell me where she is, and I may let you live." With that the men came alive and answered.

"It's the Sorcerer, he made us do it. We mean you no harm. Shannon is in the loft above you. Please don't kill us. We are trying to save our families."

"Brandon, tie them up." With that Brandon grabbed some twine and forced the men to lie on their stomachs while he bound their hands behind their backs. Groping in the dark, Thadon searched for the ladder to the loft. As he moved he could hear shuffling above. As he started up the ladder he heard a door open and the wind came howling in.

"Who is there? I am Conner and this is me barn."

"Do not fear; I am Thadon, and I come in search of men who have kidnapped my lady Shannon. I mean you no harm."

"A woman, you say, there is no woman here, just the three travelers. One is at the cottage. Why do ye say this?"

"I have tied the other two up and Shannon is hidden above. My cousin Brandon is with the two men." With that Thadon continued up the darkened ladder to the loft. Feeling his way around, he soon came upon Shannon still bound and gagged.

Untying her mouth, she cried, her voice shaking, "Thadon... Thadon, you have come at last. Please untie me; my hands are cold and I can't feel my feet. Hold me, I am cold, oh Thadon, you have found me." Quickly untying her he wrapped her in his arms and spread his wool cloak around her, kissing her passionately as he did so. "Shannon, I came as quickly as I could. These men will pay dearly for what they have done to you. I have been worried sick. I will rub your legs and feet to warm them. You are safe now. I won't let them hurt you again. Brandon, watch out for the third man."

"His name is Craig," chattered Shannon still shaking from the cold Conner exclaimed, "A woman in my loft! I am fooled, I be fooled."

"Conner, my men are staying at your cousin's cottage. He told us of you. This man Craig, is he asleep? We need to be sure that he is caught and is no danger to your family."

"Aye, the Missus died last year. I am a poor widower and now I am fooled by bad men in the night. He is asleep in front of the fire. I came out to get me jug. I didn't wish these men to find it and drink it all up.

What has the world come to? My children, my children, they are asleep with a bad man at my fire."

"Be calm, Conner, may we share your whiskey? Please may we have a drink, it will help warm Shannon. We will surprise this Craig. Your family will be safe." With that Conner lifted some straw from the floor to reveal a door in the floor. He raised it and pulled forth a corked pottery jug. Thadon and Shannon descended from the loft.

"It is me own home brew. The lady is welcome to it." With that Thadon raised the jug to Shannon's shaking lips. She gagged a few swallows down; then he too took a few swigs and handed it to Brandon who accepted it gladly before passing it back to Conner.

"Brandon, get our horses in. Conner, we will go with you to the house. Let us give Shannon a few more minutes to warm up. Are you feeling any better?"

"Aye, I can feel my legs again. Can I have more whiskey, and do you have any food here? I am very hungry." Thadon nodded and pulled a hard biscuit from his coat pocket.

"Try this, it is all I have. Conner, when we capture Craig can Shannon have some food? I have a few coins in my bags. We can pay you." Conner lowered the jug from his mouth and wiped the dribble from his beard.

"Aye, we have fresh goat cheese and bread." Taking another swallow, he passed the jug back to Shannon. "Take another swig, missy, it will warm you sure. The storm is very bad. I have an old woolen coat here for nights like this. I will get it for you." Brandon returned and led the horses into a stall with two goats. Throwing them some hay he joined the others and reached for the jug Thadon offered.

"The rain is coming in gusts. It is better if we wait."

"But; what of us? What is to become of us? We only did this to save our families," cried one of the kidnappers.

"I have heard this story from O'Toole. In the morning we will return to Conner's cousin's house. For now be quite and lay still. You have wronged this lady. I will let her decide your fate. We go soon to the cottage to capture your friend. Tell me about him. Does he too have family being held or is he one of Malroc's men?"

"He is not our friend. As Shannon has told you, his name is Craig. He is a fierce Norseman who does not like us Irish. He does not have family here. He is one of Thain's trusted men. He is strong. He led our band and will get a reward for capturing your Lady. We do not trust him. He will not be easy to overcome. Wait till he is fast asleep and surprise him if you can." Thadon nodded to Brandon as he downed another swig.

"I know of this man. He is strong and can be ruthless. Conner, will you go with us?" Conner nodded taking a long, hard swallow from the now half empty jug.

"He is a big man. I fear for my wee ones," said Conner lowering the jug.

Shannon spoke with revenge in her voice. "He is the one who tied me and threatened me if I tried to escape. Give me a knife and a club for I wish to hurt him as he hurt me."

"Are you sure you are up to a fight?"

"Aye, I am much better and I look forward to a good night's sleep. Let us knock him in the head so we can be next to the fire instead of him."

Thadon unsheathed his long sword and motioned for Brandon. "The rain is slowing. Let us be quick before he wakes." Sloshing through the wet grass, they made their way to the cottage. Thadon motioned for Brandon and Shannon to stand on either side while Conner stood back. Opening the door they found Craig waiting with sword in hand. Craig charged, roaring like a lion. Thadon rolled to the right just in time to avoid his slashing cut. Shannon saw her chance as Craig focused on Thadon. She charged him from behind and stabbed him in the shoulder with the short sword Thadon had given her. Brandon jumped on him and held his sword arm down. Howling in rage Craig cursed them. "You can't defeat him. You have no idea what you are up against. He will burn you where you stand." Thadon recovered and clubbed him viciously from the side cutting a deep gash in the side of his head. He struggled no more and lay still. Brandon got up and nodded to Thadon.

"I think he is dead."

"So be it, Shannon are you okay?"

"Aye, I am tired. I am hungry. I am cold and he is dead. Mister Conner, may we come in?" Shocked and a bit speechless Conner inclined his head, motioning them into the cottage.

Taking a deep breath Brandon said, "What should we do with his body?"

"We can drag him to Conner's hog lot and feed him to the hogs. It is what he deserves." With that Shannon stumbled into the cottage with Conner not far behind. Dragging Craig's body and then throwing it over the fence, Thadon and Brandon hurried to the cottage for some badly needed food and sleep. "Mister Conner, I wish to thank you for your help. When we conquer Eblana I will send you several kegs of whiskey."

Craig felt them drag his half conscious body and then throw him over the fence. He landed with a splash in the soft mud from the hog wallows. The impact brought him back to consciousness. He lay still trying to get his bearings. His head throbbed from the clubbing and his wounded left arm was buried in the mud. An old sow nudged him with her snout. He rolled over and pulled his boot knife from his right boot. Slashing at the sow's nose he cut her and she withdrew a few feet squealing in disgust at the outrage. Craig crawled to the fence and managed to pull himself up and over with his good right arm. He lay their panting. The mud had stopped the blood flow from his head and shoulder. Groggily he dragged himself to his feet and stumbled off downhill and away from the farmhouse. He needed to get as far from there as he could before he passed out again. After a few minutes he made it to a steep hillside with exposed rocks jutting out. Scrambling downhill he slid between two ledges. Stopping on a lower level he crawled along the outcrop and pulled himself into a grotto where he collapsed, panting from the pain.

The sun shone brightly on the wet grasses the next morning as Brandon saddled the horses. Thadon, with Shannon in tow, strode to the barn. The sun bathed their faces with a welcome warmth as they waved to Brandon and entered the barn to find the pair of abductors sitting up awaiting their fate. "Craig is dead. We fed him to the hogs. Will you swear allegiance to help us defeat Malroc and Thain?"

"We will do what we can. Can you help us rescue our families from the Sorcerer's fire? He will burn them when he finds we didn't do as he said."

"Shannon has forgiven you but you must help us and we will help you. Ride to Eblana and tell all that we come. Ask them to help us and we will help you set your families free. Will you do this?"

"The sorcerer is powerful. How will you defeat him?"

"We have a more powerful Sorcerer on our side. His name is Dante. He is meeting us soon and together we will defeat them." Thadon bent down and cut their bonds. "We go to meet our men. Ride to Eblana and tell all that we come."

CHAPTER 9
DECEIT DISCOVERED

Craig made his way to Eblana on foot and at nightfall entered his room from the outside stair above the O'Caollaidhe Tavern. Changing clothes and cleaning his wounds as best he could, he left his room and found his way to the Matron Thelda. As the head mother of the tavern women he trusted her. He knew he couldn't return to the castle without his hostage and admit his failure. He needed information about what had happened since he left. Thelda was shocked to see him "What happened to you? Have you been brawling again? No doubt over some other man's lady."

"Nay...nay; not this time. I was sent to Ossury by Thain and his Sorcerer Malroc to capture Thadon or capture a family member for some trade for a mysterious magic called a compass. It is said that this magic can guide a ship even on foggy nights when you can't see the sun. Malroc has convinced Thain that they can trade this to the Britain Romans for a ship full of gold. Thadon caught up with me and I barely escaped with my life. I need your help to patch me up. What do you know of this Malroc? Have you seen him or Thain? I need to know what has happened since I left."

"Aye; 'tis odd that you ask. This very day Thain was here in a foul mood looking for this Malroc. He left in a hurry and didn't even spend time with the ladies, which is unusual for him. We haven't seen this Malroc for a few days, but my ladies say that Helga overheard him talking with some men he hired to deliver a message to the Romans. He told them to deliver his letter to the Romans who would be landing with a large force on the coast three leagues north of Eblana. We haven't seen him since. I thought Helga must be mistaken as to what she heard What thinkest thou? Are we to be attacked and all made into Roman slaves? My girls are all scared, and now most of the town's people have heard this tale. What should we do?"

"Where is Helga? Ask her to come here, for I wish to ask her what else she heard."

"She is next door. I will see if she is finished with her man. Wait here; I'll be right back with some fresh water and bandages for your head and arm."

"Bring me some bread and meat also. Here are some coins for your trouble." Snatching the coins Thelda left and soon returned with Helga. Between mouthfuls of bread and meat Craig was soon bandaged and feeling much better as the ladies finished wrapping his wounds. "Helga, tell me exactly what you heard."

"Am I in trouble? I want no trouble from this man. He scares me. All the ladies are afraid of him. Are ye working for him too?"

"I was, but not now. I want no part of being a Roman slave again. I was not told of an invasion. You are in no more trouble that the rest of us. Tell me exactly what ye heard."

"Well, I was in the room next door to them and the walls are thin. I had been resting when I awoke to their voices. He, this Malroc, made the men swear allegiance to him and not Thain. I was spooked but I couldn't move for fear that he would hear me. He told them that soon Thain would be fighting Thadon and that the Romans would come in after the battle and take over. He told them to deliver a note to the Romans who would be landing on the coast three leagues north. He promised them that he would take care of them and that soon he would be very rich. He promised them more gold. They were to return to him with the Roman answer. They were to meet him at the old Monks Ruins northwest of town."

Munching more bread and chasing it with the beer Thelda had brought, Craig mused on this information. "A double cross: Malroc has been using Thain and by pitting brother against brother he seeks to weaken us so the Romans can conquer us. This must have been his plan all along. I believe it was he who poisoned Eric. I saw him burn men with the flick of his hands. He is an evil Sorcerer and is not to be trusted. I must get to Thain and warn him of this deceit. We need to stop the battle between the brothers if we are to survive. We must tell this tale to all who will listen. Helga, will you go with me to meet with Thain?"

Helga looked to Thelda, "What should I do? I am scared. I am just a working girl. Thain won't believe me."

" I will go with you. Before those men left, they spent some of their coins at the Tavern and I have saved them. I kept them since they were different. I will show them to Thain. Maybe he will believe then." With that they left in Thelda's buggy and were soon at Thain's castle.

Thain listened intently as Craig told his story and then had the women tell theirs. "Let me see these coins." Thelda handed over two of the coins. Thain studied them. "These are quite old. Older than any coins I have seen before. You say these men paid you these and that they came from Malroc."

"Aye, I saved them as I had never seen their kind before."

"These men, do you know them?"

"Nay, they are strangers. Travelers from the north, I believe, as their talk sounded as men from far away." With that Thain stood and then began pacing back and forth. Reaching into his tunic he withdrew several coins and handed them to Thelda.

"Take these in return for the others. I wish to keep them. Return to your tavern and watch for these men to return. Send word to me if you see them or any new strangers in town. Craig, come with me. We have much to discuss." Craig nodded to the women and then followed Thain. Moving to the cellar Thain grabbed a jug of whiskey. "This I will need to get me through the night. I have been played for a fool. Malroc was just using me, baiting me with stories of power and wealth. My life is forfeit. Which is worse: being a Roman Slave, or kneeling before my brother?" Taking a long slow gulp of the bronze liquor, Thain paced back and forth. Tomorrow I intend to go to Thadon and his men and admit to them that I have been under the control of a Sorcerer. Now that he has been gone for the last two days I have had a lot of time to reflect on these past weeks. I have no desire to fight Thadon over this land. There is plenty of land for both of us. You have been present when Malroc was around. How did he do this to me? Did you see him do anything to me that changed me? "

"May I have a snort of that jug?" Thain took another snort and then passed it over.

"I indeed saw him do that to you many times," said Craig as he wiped the dribble from his beard.

Thain continued pacing, "but how? What did he do?"

"He would walk up to you and past you and as he passed he would wave his hand and you would change what you were saying and say what he just said."

"You saw this and didn't tell me."

"This is the first time I have been with you without him around. Besides, I saw what he could do with the flick of his wrist, and I really didn't wish to challenge him. You are different now. I can tell you the truth. Before, when you were under his influence, I didn't dare for fear of my life." Reaching for the jug, Thain cleared his throat and spat at the fireplace.

"This is difficult to accept and makes me guilty of doing nothing when Father died. He was sick when I agreed to let Malroc tend to him, but not so sick that he should have died. I see now that Malroc poisoned him and made me believe that he died naturally. I was fooled and now must admit it, but I'll be dammed if I'll let him do this double cross. The Romans are our greatest enemy, and now that they are here at his request, I have no choice but to surrender to Thadon.

CHAPTER 10
ON TO EBLANA

The sun was bright and the countryside beautiful as Thadon and his troop rode to Conner's cousin's home and rejoined their men. Saralynn cried as she hugged Shannon. The men cheered. "Let us ride to meet Shane and our men. I for one am tired of sleeping in the cold. Let us gather our men and ride to meet Dante."

Thadon lit the huge stack of deadwood. Soon it blazed brightly and the men threw more wood on top till the fire reached to the sky. The winds had picked up and the sparks flew high into the dark night sky, filling the void like thousands of fireflies. "Look, to the north; its Dante's signal. He has made it!" exclaimed Shane.

"There, over there, more fires," shouted Brandon, pointing northwest and west. Thadon smiled for the first time in days.

"It has begun. Tomorrow we fight. Remember the plan. Set the trap as Dante said. We must be strong, change ourselves into demons eight feet tall and cut our way thru to Dante on the other side. There he will fight and defeat this Malroc who with his dark magic would enslave us all." Pulling his sword and holding it high Thadon screamed at the starry sky like an avenging eagle. "Aiee, it is our time to stand together as one people and unite all of Ireland so that we may sing, dance, live on our green land and raise our families as the free Irish of old. Tonight we sing and dance and bring the Wee Folk out to play. With their magic we shall endure." Thrusting his sword into his scabbard he walked to Shannon and offered her his hand. Picking her up Thadon turned, "Music, music, sound the Tin Whistle, strike your fiddles and dance like you've never danced before." Spinning on his toes he wheeled Shannon around and around till all began to dance around the flames of the giant fire.

Malroc arose from his studies of the ancient Tome. Soon he would have what he wanted. The Briton Romans had sent a courier accepting his terms for the Compass. They would arrive tomorrow and end this petty fight between two brothers. His plan was finally coming together. With all that Roman gold and the promise of the rule of this pathetic Irish Island, he could finally conquer Dante and be free from his old enemy. This time he would prevail. With the brothers fighting each other and decimating each other's forces, it will be simple for the Romans to step in and take control. Finally the Irish have something that the Romans needed. They would not stop until they acquired the Compass. His letter to the Roman Praetor describing his plan to delay Thain and keep him here until Thadon and Dante arrived was working. Thain had no clue. He smiled in anticipation of the upcoming ambush.

Creidon walked along the foredeck of the Noria. Dante had asked him to wait there for two days then bring the boats up the mouth of the Liffey River and dock the boats at the Wood Quay. Nightfall was coming in as he looked out to Sea. What he saw staggered him back. Ships, Roman ships. Sounding the alarm, he called to his men to raise anchors. The Roman ships were moving into a harbor north of them for the night. Frantically he roused his men and soon they were under way skimming along the shoreline. He had to warn Dante. This would change everything. With the Romans coming all could be lost. This fight between Thadon and Thain was trivial compared to the threat of Roman occupation. Having escaped from slavery in England as a small boy he knew all to well what was at stake. Looking back he saw that John on the Banth was also well under way. Having only a few men for each boat made their progress slow, he had no choice but to row all night if he was to beat the Romans to Eblana. Why were they coming now; and so many? He counted at least four warships before they had entered the cove and was out of sight.

Creidon finally beached the warboats northeast of Eblana, hiding them in a quiet cove. He left most of his crew with the boats, taking only two men with him to find Dante. Giving the men instructions to row away if the Romans came, but stay and wait for Dante if they didn't, they set out. Traveling at night they soon reached a hilltop wherein they could see a large fire ahead. They found Dante talking with his men. "Dante, it is I, Creidon. The Romans are coming." With that said and the tale soon told, Dante ordered the men to set out now to skirt the town and rejoin Thadon. Thain was not their biggest concern now. The Romans were.

Thain and Craig watched the fires on the hills surrounding Eblana. "It must be Thadon, come for his revenge. With the news that you have given me of Malroc's deceit, and the coming of this Roman Army, I must swallow my pride and ride out to Thadon and warn him of this danger to us all. Will you accompany me?"

"Thadon left me for dead in a hog lot. I kidnapped his woman. Art thou sure you want me with you? He surely hates who and what I am."

"I will tell him the truth. All of it, including Malroc poisoning our Father and my doing nothing. I know now that I was a vain fool to listen to the lies of such as Malroc. He played on my jealous pride. I will give myself up to Thadon to do with me as he wishes for I would rather have him ruling this land than the Romans. I did nothing while my father died, and I am guilty of the worst of crimes for believing the words of the deceiver. It is he I will now defeat by going to Thadon and confessing my sins. He wished for our armies to fight each other so that the Romans could easily defeat us. By going now to Thadon with a white flag and admitting my part in all this, then and only then can I have revenge against Malroc, for if all our people fight together, Norsemen and Irishmen alike we can win this war and drive this evil bastard from our lands."

"If thou will do all this, then I too will join you and turn myself over to Thadon."

"Help me gather some of the gold we stole from the Romans. I will give it to Thadon to pay his men. I hope it will help convince him that we are sincere in joining him in this fight. Morning will be here soon. Meet me at the front gate with three horses at dawn. I will bring the gold and maybe Thadon will listen."

Thadon looked out over the dawning day to a strange sight. Clearly off to his right must be Dante coming with the one hundred men and to his left came two riders leading a third horse straight from Eblana under a white flag. Shannon came up beside him and hooked her arm into his. "What is happening? Dante was supposed to wait until Thain came charging out, and who are these men on horses under a white flag?"

"I don't know. Go get the others up and tell Mother to come. She should be here to see and hear what they have to say."

Dante could see the two riders heading toward Thadon, so he spurred the horse he had acquired from a local farmer into a gallop and was amazed when he recognized Thain. Pulling up along side him, he nodded. "Well, I see that you are not dead after all."

"No not yet, but soon we all may be. I go to make peace with Thadon, for the Romans are coming."

"Ah, yes, so you have heard as we have that they are just north of town. Is their coming your doing and are you still in league with this Malroc?"

Thain took a deep breath and exhaled slowly, "Let us meet with Thadon. I must tell him myself of the upcoming danger and my part in all this. As I see you are just arriving, did you bring the magic compass? That is what Malroc has brought the Romans for. He has promised them your compass in exchange for a ship load of gold. Is it true? Can you guide a ship even in the darkest of nights or the worst of storms?"

Dante's left eyebrow raised as he pondered Thain and this sudden change in events. "Let us not keep the others waiting. I truly look forward to hearing all that you have to say." Motioning for Thain to continue he nudged his horse into a trot.

Thadon could not believe his eyes. He pulled his sword, "You killed our Father and you dare come to me with a white flag. Get down off your horse and defend yourself, for you have wronged me for the last time."

"Hold on, Thadon." Dante dismounted first. "We must hear what he has to say. We have a far more dangerous enemy on our doorstep. A legion of Roman soldiers is just north of town."

"I don't care, and that man with him is Craig. He kidnapped Shannon and I thought I had killed him. Get down now, before I have my archers put arrows through you."

Dropping the reins, Thain spoke, "I have come because I have been a fool, and yes, I am guilty of doing nothing when Father was poisoned. Craig is guilty of everything you say, but he was doing so following Malroc's devious plans. We have come to you to give ourselves over to you to do with as you wish, but first hear me out. A far greater danger than I is coming. Malroc's plan was for you and me to fight and kill off all our people so that the Romans could come in and capture Dante and steal his compass. This whole ordeal is about this magic compass which I know nothing of." Looking to Dante he asked," Is it true? Is there such a magic? Is it worth all the lives of the Norsemen and Irish alike? Before I die I would like to know."

All eyes now turned to Dante. "Get down Thain and Craig. Let us sit and talk. We must prepare if we are to meet this threat. Thadon put up your sword. Last night Criedon came to me to warn me of the Romans. He has seen them. That is why I am here. Now is not the time for vengeance but for planning. Let us put our disputes aside and hear the rest of their story. Malroc is the one behind all this, as I suspected all along. He will do anything to get the compass, including selling us all out to the Romans."

They sat in a great circle with Thain being the first to speak. "I am the worst of fools, for I have allowed myself to be deceived. I take full responsibility for the death of our aging Father who was in ill health when I allowed Malroc to tend him. Instead of healing him as he said, he poisoned him and he died. I know that now. He then convinced me that I should capture you and hold you to keep back a challenge to Fathers estate. He knew exactly how to manipulate me. He played to my vanity. Luckily you escaped, and I applaud you. I am here today to tell you that Malroc's real intention was to cause inner turmoil and war between brothers to weaken us. He seeks the Magic Compass to sell to the Romans. Craig came to me last night with women from the O'Caollaidhe Tavern who overheard Malroc sending men to deliver a note to the Romans. He gave them gold coins which they spent in Thelda's brothel. I have these coins." With that he produced the coins and pitched them to Thadon and Dante sitting next to each other. "These are very old coins. I have not seen their kind before. Hearing all this Craig and I have come to you under a white flag with the gold I stole from the Romans. It is here on the pack horse for you and your men. Our common enemy has always been the Britain Romans and now they are here. We surrender ourselves to you with but one wish; that we be allowed to fight alongside you to defeat our enemy. If we live through the fight, I ask that we be allowed to go by sea to our Fathers Norse homeland never to return. I have spoken." With that he nodded to Dante and Thadon and sat down.

Dante examined the coins and then stood. "These coins are very old indeed and could only have come from Malroc. He has indeed played Thain for a fool, and we all morn the loss of Eric. We can turn the tables on him now that Thain has boldly come forward. He is correct. Your enemies are the Britain Romans and Malroc, for they would enslave all of you. It is up to Thadon to decide what punishment Thain and Craig must be dealt for their crimes against you. I for one agree that they should be allowed to bring all their men and ours together to fight this threat. The Romans wait for our fight before they attack, hoping that we will kill ourselves. Listening to all this I have come up with a plan to foil Malroc and the Romans. Creidon has told me that their warboats are anchored in a bay northeast of Eblana. They have left a small force with their ships. If Thadon and Thain join forces and fortify themselves along the south shore of the Liffey River at the Wood Quay and show the Romans a unified force, they will be confused and be forced to rethink their attack. This will give me time to row with one hundred men and capture their warboats. If there is any gold aboard, we can promise it to our men and the people of Eblana to fight along with us. If we are successful, we can turn the Romans against Malroc hiding in his lair and trade them the Warboats in return for peace. This is and yet isn't about the Compass. The Britain Romans have tried many times to conquer and enslave you. This is just one more time to try and control you and stop you from raiding their shores as you so often do. Even if we gave them my Compass, they would turn against you and slaughter you anyway. Thain has given us a chance to force them to surrender and not fight or to destroy them if we must fight. I would prefer that none of you die in this battle. If we engage them many will die or be maimed. We can capture their warboats. Without them they cannot return to their homeland. The key is their boats. We will attack them at night while they sleep and one by one steal their boats or burn them. I ask that all of you consider this for it will turn the tide against them. I have spoken." With that he nodded to Thadon and Thain and sat down.

Thadon stood and looked at all seated for a long moment before he spoke. Focusing on Thain he nodded to him and to Craig and then his Mother who had just joined them. "My heart is full of hope for the first time in many moons. Up until now I could only wonder as

MEN OF THE COMPASS

to the outcome of this fight. My brother has come forth and humbled himself before us. I did not expect this, but I welcome the opportunity to fight alongside him against our old enemy. I am half Norse and half Irish but I was born here and this is my Island as it is yours. If we fight them, many will die as Dante has said. We must outthink them and turn things around as Dante has suggested. If his plan doesn't work, then we fight for our very existence. Let us march now to Eblana and gather all who can and will fight with us. Let us dig down deep into our Irish and Norse souls and change into demons standing ten feet tall and scream at them to leave our land or die." With that he drew his sword and screamed, "AIEEE"

    Malroc watched the fires burn on the hills surrounding Eblana and smiled. These simple Irish and Norsemen were so easy to manipulate. Soon they would be fighting each other as they always did. Sitting down at the long table, he unfolded the ancient Tome he had brought with him. In it was the collective knowledge of the ancient order of the Druids. He had killed many to obtain this book. It gave him power over the inferior beings whose lives he detested. Tomorrow he would reap the fruits of his schemes. Now he must perfect his powers, for the upcoming fight with his old enemy Calcullen would not be easy. He had faced him before and barely escaped with his life. This time would be different. While Calcullen was busy fighting the Britain Romans, he would attack him from behind. That would give him the advantage he needed. He would get close enough while Calcullen was distracted and send the dreaded Druid fire. He studied the Tome all through the night and as the sun rose he moved to the upper room of the half ruined stone tower where he could observe the upcoming battle safe and away from any harm.

    Expecting to see Thain and his men marching out to engage Thadon, he was taken aback by what he saw. Two riders leading a third horse under a white flag were riding out of Eblana towards Thadon's camp. Farther out on the eastern horizon he could see a large force of men moving in the same direction. Were these Thain's men? From this distance he couldn't tell. Was Thain using a ploy to try and outflank Thadon? Engrossed by the unfolding scene before him he paced back and forth. Soon the riders went behind the hills and he couldn't see them anymore. Something was amiss. Seething in anger, he left the tower and sought his new apprentice Balfour. "Mount a horse and sneak out to the southern hills and spy on what is happening. Do not be seen and report back to me. Return in two hours and do not fail me or I will burn you to ashes. Now go and be my eyes." Bowing low Balfour backed away from his new master and scurried away.

What was it that Malroc wanted him to discover and report? Malroc scared him when he was in these moods as he so often was. It had been two weeks since he had accepted apprenticeship with Malroc, and as he saddled his mare, he questioned again why he had accepted Malroc's offer. The more he saw of this man the more he was scared of him and this morning was the worst. Yesterday he had watched as Malroc punished Johnathon, his servant, for not bringing him the wine he had asked for. It was terrible and the man would possibly be crippled for life due to his burns from Malroc's hands. Enough was enough. Why not just ride out to Thadon and turn on Malroc and join Thadon's band? After all, they were his people and if not for Malroc's gold he would not have agreed to be Malroc's assistant. Kicking his mare harder he decided to ride straight to Thadon and tell him all he knew.

Rising from the circle of allies Thain pointed out to the west, "Rider coming in." All eyes turned to see the young man riding hard to their camp. Pulling up hard on his horse, the young man dismounted and strode to the circle of men. Thain recognized him. "Balfour, what are ye doing here? Art thou still Malroc's apprentice or has thou come to fight on our side?"

Bewildered for a second Balfour looked at Thain and then at Thadon. "You are together. Art thou brothers again and not enemies? Tell me this is true. I have ridden to join you, but I never expected to find you together. Malroc must be defeated for he is cruel and evil. He sent me here to spy on you, but I feared for my life. I come to you asking that you allow me to join you, for I can no longer work for him."

Thain embraced him and then turned to Thadon. "Here is a sign that we are on the right path. Tell us what you know of Malroc. Where is he, and what is he planning?"

"He is in the old Monks Ruin at the hill northwest of Town. He is in a foul mood. He thought you would be killing each other by now. Boy is he gonna be mad when he finds out you are together."

Dante stepped forward. "Welcome, young Balfour; my name is Dante. Come with me, as I have questions to ask you. Thadon, Thain, it is time to mount your horses and ride and run to your defenses on the Liffey River. I will spend a few moments with this young man and then I will leave for the boats. Thadon, pick the men you wish to go with me, and I will be along soon."

"Balfour, tell me of Malroc. How many men does he have near him?"

"He is alone, except for old Johnathon, but Johnathon was burned by Malroc last night. There art no others. Last evening, Malroc burned Johnathon for bringing him the wrong wine. He is a vengeful and hateful man. I feared for my life. I am happy to be here. It pleases me that Thain has also come to his senses and is here with Thadon. What can I do to help?"

"You have done much already but I need you to be our eyes and ears to spy on Malroc. Can you do this without being seen?"

"Aye, I can hide in the rocks northwest of the Ruins. What does thou wish for me to do?"

"Do not go near to him again. He can do mind control if you are close to him. Stay hidden and report to Thadon and Thain if Malroc moves from the ruin. Can you shoot a bow?"

"Aye, why do you ask?"

"You can defend yourself against him with the bow and arrow if he discovers you. He can deflect an arrow with his powers but it will weaken him from the effort if you keep shooting. He has to focus on the path of the arrow to deflect it from hitting him. Take two others with you and space them apart from you. If he discovers you and comes after you, the three of you should shoot as fast as you can then ride away and find Thadon or Thain and tell him that Malroc has emerged. I do not wish for him to sneak behind them while they are watching the Romans across the River. Can you do this?"

"Aye, I can do this, is there anything else?"

"Yes, have you seen him at night? Does he read from a large leather bound book that looks very old?"

"Yes, it is on his table and he calls it a Tome. He promised to teach me from it if I showed talent, but he never did."

"Thank you young Balfour. Let us go to the brothers and tell them that you will watch him. Pick two men to go with you and stay hidden. If he leaves and has not discovered you, send the other two to report to the Thadon and Thain. Wait till he is far away and then steal this book for me if you can. Before you touch the book, sprinkle some of this bag of powder on it and it will diffuse any spells that he has placed on it. Wrap it in a blanket with the powder still on it and it will keep the spell from returning. It is light sensitive, so keep it wrapped. Do not attempt to open it. Keep it bundled, and let no one have it except Thadon. He will reward you for bringing this book to him."

They found Thadon and Thain and told them of Balfour's mission to watch Malroc and report to them if he moved toward them. Taking Thadon aside Dante spoke softly, "I have asked him to steal the ancient Tome, if Malroc leaves without it. It is the book of knowledge of the Druids. I suspected that Malroc had stolen it, and Balfour has seen him reading from it. I have given Balfour a bag of spell dissolver powder to sprinkle on it before he touches it. If he brings this book to you do not open it without me there. If something happens to me and Balfour doesn't bring the book to you, make every effort to obtain it. If you get this book; keep it safe until you recover my possessions at your Mother's home. In them you will find my book of spells. Study them well before you attempt to open the Tome. Those two books hold all my knowledge including the secret of the Compass. If I do not survive this fight I ask that you carry on my work and learn the Druid sleep for it will take decades of practice to reach an understanding of the powers contained in our order. I wished to teach all of this to you before now but there has been little time. Take this bag of powder. If you can recover this book sprinkle the powder over it then wrap the book in a blanket and keep it from the light as it is light sensitive. I would go after this book now if I could but there is no time. It is important that we recover this book if we can."

"I will do as you ask. The men are ready. Your men are waiting on the lee side of the hill. How will I know that you have captured the warboats?"

"I will sound the drums. A long roll then three fast beats will mean that I have succeeded and will join you soon. Listen for the drums; then send this note by arrow to the Romans. It will buy us some time to arrive and reinforce you." With that he handed Thadon a folded note. "Good luck to you, young cousin. Time is just starting for you. Practice your lessons while I am away. If Malroc finds you, pretend that you are weak until he gets very close then lash out with the power of the fire. It will catch him unaware. Have your men shoot as many arrows at him as fast as they can. He can deflect them but he must focus on their path, and this will eventually weaken him. He is not easily defeated, but he is mortal, and arrows can kill him. Tell the others this story and be on guard. He may come after you to disrupt our plans. He will disguise himself so that you don't recognize him. Most likely he will look like a poor cripple, cloaked in heavy cloth with a wood staff. Tell the others to be watchful for someone as I have described. If he gets close to you he will exert mind control to slow your reflexes. Remember your lessons and close your mind to him by concentrating on his hands not his eyes. Do not look into his eyes. You are the one he is most likely to come after, thinking he could trade you for my Compass. Keep Brandon, Shane, Brian and Shawn around you at all times and tell them to arm themselves with bow and arrow as well as long swords. Tell them what I have told you and it may save their lives. Be watchful, and I will return as soon as I can. If I catch the Roman boat guards on land at night around a camp fire as I hope, we will surround them and be back here in two days. If I haven't returned in two days, send the note anyway. We will at the least be able to cripple their boats and sink some of them. The note will force them to send a large force back to the ships to try and retake them. That way there will be fewer men for you to fight and they may be willing to negotiate. Lie to them and tell them you have more men than you do. Spread your forces out along the Wood Quay and light large fires at night and scream at them like the Wild Irish that you are. Tell them to go home, that you have nothing they want. Delay them as long as you can. I have sent Balfour and two others to watch over Malroc and report to you if he moves. Tomorrow, send new men to relieve them. They will be hidden in the rock ledges on the hillside northwest of the Ruin."

"What if they attack tomorrow?"

"Pull your bows tight and shoot volleys of fire arrows into them, then retreat behind cover and fire more arrows. Burn their boats as they try and cross the River. Fight a delaying fight. Let your middle collapse and draw them into your middle. You will then have three sides to fire into them. Do not attack them in formation. That is what they want you to do. Keep drawing back and do not directly engage them. They are better armed and trained to fight in tight formations. At night, harass them, then pull back and hit them from the sides. Keep killing or wounding as many as you can without going sword to sword. After losing many men you will have forced them to fortify themselves in the buildings you have left behind. After the first day, call to them and tell them you have captured their ships. Send the note if you can. This will cause them to slow down and split their forces. That will give me a day's head start on attacking their boats."

"We will do as you say. I will watch for Malroc. I will tell Thain and the men what you have said. Thank you for all that you have done, and return to me, as I have many questions unanswered."

Dante embraced and smiled at him, then mounted his horse and disappeared over the hill.

CHAPTER 11

DEFENDING THE HOMELAND

Thain manned the men on the south half while Thadon took the north half of the Wood Quay riverfront. Thadon could smell the smoke from the Roman camps as evening came on and the wind blew steadily from the northwest. His mind played on all the possibilities of the attack to come. How many were there? How long would they wait? He hated this waiting game but he must do it to give Dante time to attack their ships. Malroc; the thought of him lying in wait for Thain and him to kill each other gave him a sense of strength now that Thain had come to his senses. Once Malroc had left Thain he no longer had mind control over him. Maybe it was just the luck of the Irish or the Wee Folk had intervened. He was glad that Thain was no longer his enemy. Maybe he should take men and attack Malroc in his lair. Dante didn't suggest that but he did say obtain the Tome if he could. He fingered the bag of Powder that Dante had given him. He hated Malroc and thought of all the ways he could torture him and prolong his death. A quick death would be too good for him for all the things he had done. His mind drifted to Shannon and his Mother, whom he had left with the Conner family until this battle was over. It took a lot of convincing, but finally they had agreed to stay behind, for it was there that the men would retreat to if the Romans got the upper hand. Darkness was setting in, and he missed them even more.

The cool winds blew across the faces of the three watchers as the sun set over the hills. Crouched low against the rock outcrops they kept their vigil on the old Monk Ruins where Malroc had set up his abode. They all straightened and looked at one another as Malroc emerged from the old stable area mounted on the black gelding. He was dressed all in black with a hood over his head and he carried a long staff. Balfour whispered to his fellow watchers. "Follow him but do not get to close. Find Thadon or Thain and tell them he is coming their way." They nodded and slowly moved to their horses, grazing behind the hilltop. Balfour watched as they rode slowly down the hill towards the Ruin. When they had passed the ruin Balfour picked up the extra blanket and headed downhill. This was his time to get revenge on Malroc. With the powder Dante had given him he was determined to steal the Ancient Book of Druid Spells and collect the reward Dante had promised that Thadon would give him. He entered the stable area and picked up the heavy hammer and iron bar he knew were there. He entered the old courtyard and opened the door to the kitchen. From there he moved to the locked door of the tower. Beyond that door lay the stairs to the upper room, which was still intact and had a good roof. It was there that Malroc slept and where he had last seen the book. Walking up to the door he took out the bag of powder that Dante had given him. Sprinkling it on the iron lock he gasped as it glowed briefly then dimmed. Malroc had put a spell on it. Cold chills ran down his spine at the thought of what would have happened to him without the powder. Inserting the bar into the lock he twisted with all his youthful strength. Many hours spent laboring at the blacksmith's forge had toughened him, and he snapped the rusted hinges freeing the lock. Cautiously he pushed the door open then looked in. Moonlight drifted through the windows and he waited as his eyes adjusted to the darkness. Seeing the stairway, he moved to it and climbed to the upper room. He scanned the room and saw the book on the table, still open. Glancing left and right he slowly moved to the book. Standing a few feet away he tossed some powder on it and involuntarily jumped back as the powder gave off an eerie glow as it slowly rose floating over the book in the moonlight. Taking another fistful of powder he sprinkled it all over the book. It glowed briefly then dimmed. Taking the blanket out, he spread it over the book and closed it, then finished wrapping it all the way around. Turning, he made his way down the stairs and out into the courtyard and the fields beyond. Making his way up the hills, he returned to the rock outcrops. Sinking down on his knees, he pondered what to do. Should he dare keep the book with him or hide it and come back for it after all the fighting was over? Looking around, he explored the ledge and soon found what he was looking for. A small grotto with a dirt floor would provide a dry hiding place. He crawled back into the deep ledge area and with his sword dug a hole and inserted the book, still wrapped in the blanket. He placed some thin ledge stones in on top of it then covered it all over with the dirt and smoothed it all out.

Malroc watched from his hiding place behind the rock outcrops as the two riders approached. His wariness and suspicions had warned him that he was being followed. Reaching out with his mind as they neared, he sensed their tracking of him. He listened as they discussed the horse tracks they were following. "He went this way. The tracks lead toward those rocks." Sending his mind into theirs, he soothed their fears as they looked to each other and continued on towards him. When they were close enough he lashed out with the Druid fire, catching them unawares. Their horses reared and threw them to the ground then bolted away. Both men frantically jumped to their feet and ran, which only fanned the flames. In a short distance both men fell screaming to their knees, consumed by the fire which enveloped their clothes. Shrugging disgustedly, Malroc mounted the waiting gelding and slowly made his way towards town, his senses heightened now that his suspicions were confirmed. His devious plans had evidently been discovered. The battle of the brothers had not occurred. If they were together they would be difficult to defeat. He must find out. The whores in town would know. Making his way slowly towards town he fell in behind other riders coming in for the night. The other riders looked back, but seeing no danger they continued on. As they neared the first buildings Malroc veered off and dismounted behind a shed. Tying his horse he pulled his hood over his head and with his staff hobbled off as a poor crippled beggar looking for a handout. As he shambled he sent his senses out. Probing the minds of the people he passed he sought out the danger he knew must lie ahead. He pulled himself into a darkened doorway and listened. All was quiet, too quiet. He watched as an old woman came his way carrying a large basket. In his most sincere voice Malroc called to her, "Hello Madam, could ya help a poor traveler find a place to stay for the night? I can pay. I am hungry and tired and look forward to a warm fire."

The old women, burdened with her heavy load, turned at the sound of his voice. Frightened at first, her fears were calmed by his smooth voice which seemed gentle. " 'Tis no place empty. All rooms are taken. The town is full of fightin' men. A battle is coming. Best be on your way if ye wish to stay alive. The Romans are across the Liffey and the brothers

Thadon and Thain and their men are scattered along the waterfront. It is not safe here. Leave while you can still walk." She continued walking as she talked and was soon around the corner. Leaving the doorway he headed back the way he had come. As he passed a barn he paused in the shadows. A lone rider was coming in. Peering out from his hiding place, Malroc recognized Balfour. The apprentice had not returned to him as he was instructed and now he would pay. Waiting till he was close, he threw his staff with pent up vengeance at the unsuspecting youth. With a killing blow to the side of his head Balfour fell from his horse, which panicked and galloped off. Grabbing him by his robe, he pulled him to the dark side of the building. Sensing a power emanating from the now dead apprentice he searched him and found the half empty bag of powder. Smelling it he knew he had been betrayed. Spell dissolver. It could only have come from Calcullen. Wishing now that he had not been so quick to punish, he sat back and pondered this riddle.

Thadon watched the old woman carrying the large basket of fruit and called to her to come over. "Do ye know of any rooms where my men can sleep?"

"I'll tell you like I told the crippled man with the staff, there are no rooms. All are taken"

Thadon regarded her with a puzzled look on his face, "a crippled man with a staff?"

"Aye, he called to me from the shadows, scared me at first, wanted to know if there were any rooms. Strange that he didn't know what is going on, everyone knows. Him hiding in the shadows that way spooked me so's I kept on me way."

"He was hiding? Did he show his face?"

"I could not see his face; he had a hood over it."

Thadon pulled back and stared out into the night. Malroc: could this man be him disguised as Dante foretold? Turning away and motioning for the woman to continue on her way he called to Brian and the others around him. "Send a runner to Thain to come at once. I believe Malroc is here and we must be wary and ready."

Night was falling and the clouds were gathering, obscuring the faint rays of dusk and giving the evening an ominous feeling as Dante signaled Creidon to pull the Banth along side the Noria and drop anchors. Soon they were shuttled onto land and set off towards the

Roman encampments. Darkness would be their ally as they neared the fires of the Romans burning brightly on the high rock outcrop area above the beach and their anchored warboats. He counted six fires with sitting men around each one, their shadows flickering from the fires. Leaving his men back behind him a short distance, he silently slipped near enough to the camps to cast a spell of drowsiness and fatigue into the minds of the unsuspecting Romans. He watched from his perch behind the trees as more and more of the men stretched out and lay down. A full moon was just breaking through the clouds as Dante returned to his men with instructions to fan out and surround the now sleeping men. "Walk silently through and take their weapons if you can, then surround them and I will wake them one by one. Take the ropes we brought and tie their feet and hands and gag them." One by one all twenty five men were tied and gagged then Dante awoke them with a spell of dream like awakening which kept them groggy. "Awake; ye men of Rome; do not struggle. You have been conquered, and if you wish to live, listen closely. Much is at stake in this struggle, most of which ye know nothing of. I give you a choice. You can die now or accept my terms. Nod if ye wish to live." Watching closely as the men quit struggling against their bonds; Dante nodded to Creidon and motioned him to be ready. One by one the men nodded and accepted their fate. As men of hire often do, they recognized who was in control. "The warboats anchored here. How many men are still on board? The first to answer my question gets a gold coin and a chance for freedom." Several men squirmed against their bonds and Dante strode to the huge red bearded man whose eyes said he wished to talk and untied his gag.

"Dante, I am Strongarm, does thou not remember me? I fought along side thee against the Normans. I have no loyalty to the Romans except their gold. It has been a long time, and I for one am glad you are here. There are but 10 men on each boat. Why did you leave England? I would have gone with you if you had asked me."

"Ah, it has indeed been a long time my old friend. Cut him loose. Ten men you say. Will you help me capture the boats? We wish no fight with the Romans. We wish for them to row back to England and leave us alone. Will ye help me?" Strongarm smiled and nodded his consent. "How many others wish to live as Strongarm?" Half a dozen

D.J. Ruckman

men squirmed against their bonds. "Strongarm. Which of these men can I trust?"

"Wilhelm, Justin, Boden, Mickdale, Chance and Bailey, they are mercenaries as I. They will welcome the chance to be on your side. We did not know it was thee who we were to go to war against. They told us we would capture a great treasure. What treasure awaits us?"

"Strongarm, untie those who I can trust. I will tell you later what all of this is about. Now, we must capture the warboats. Will ye go with me and call out to the boats so that we can board safely?"

"Aye, we are tired of this waiting around." Untying the others, Strongarm said, "On your knees. Pledge your allegiance to Dante. He is a wizard of powers beyond all that ye know. He saved my life twice, and I owe him greatly as now you do. Do you swear him your allegiance?"

All said, "Aye."

"Very well, I will spare your lives but you must help me secure yon ships." All nodded their agreement. "Creidon, leave the others tied up and put guards to watch them. Man the long boats; step lively gents, we have lots to do. I wish to be out to sea soon. Thadon will need our help. As we near the boats, I will cast a spell on them to put them to sleep if they are not already." It took the rest of the night to secure all six boats, and as morning came Dante had the ships under way to Eblana.

Thain slid off his grey stallion and landed at few feet from Thadon. "He is here? Have you seen him?" Thadon stepped back and gestured for Thain to sit down.

"An old woman told me of a man whom I believe to be Malroc. She met him on the outskirts of north town. The Romans are set in for the night. Come with me and let us see if indeed this is Malroc. If he is still about, you can tell me if it is him.

"What chance do we have against him? He can control a man's mind as he did mine. He can set a man on fire. What plan do you have to defeat him?"

"Watch and learn." Thadon turned to the pile of straw against the hillside. Focusing, he sent a wave of energy outwards and the pile burst into flames. Astonished, Thain stepped back and regarded Thadon with renewed respect.

"How; how did you do that?"

"Dante taught me. He is a Druid Master and Malroc's superior when it comes to controlling the forces of nature. He has made me his apprentice. He is my uncle on my Mother's side. We have a common ancestor named Emolac, who ventured west across the sea to Newfoundland. He left us a map which Dante and I will use to guide us to Newfoundland once this Malroc and his Roman allies are defeated. I cannot defeat Malroc alone. I need your help. Together we stand a chance of killing him or at least driving him off. Water yourself down. Wet your clothes. If it is him, guard yourself against doubt of your friends. He will try and control your mind. If I can get close enough, I will set him on fire. You and the others can shoot as many arrows as you can at him. He can deflect these but will soon tire of focusing on them. He is mortal and can be killed but has survived for many, many years. Think of Father when you fight him." Thadon reached into his robe and brought out the bag of powder that Dante had given him. "Stand still and I will sprinkle this spell dissolver on thee. Brandon, Shane, Shawn and Brian, kneel down and receive this powder. Dante said it would protect us against spells." Sprinkling the fine powder over each, he retied the bag and stored the remainder in his robe. "Let us go slowly and stay together in the shadows. He will be doing the same so we must be like ghosts if we are to find him."

Hidden on the dark side of a wood barn, Malroc's anger boiled at the thought of being outdone. He detested hiding. He feared only one man, and the mere thought of Calcullen sent waves of bitter hatred through his mind. Lashing out, he sent the Druid fire into the wood building. Stepping back he knew now what he must do. Burn the bastards. Burn the whole damn town down. Walking to the next building he sent more fire into it. He smiled as he heard screams from those inside. He continued to the next and again sent the fire.

Thain touched Thadon on the shoulder and pointed west, "Fire! It must be Malroc. He's setting fires to burn us out." They could now hear the screams of town folk running their way and yelling for help. They ran through a dark alley and halted when they saw Malroc standing in the cobblestone road and sending the fire into the next wooden cottage. Thain led their charge, venting all of his pent up energy, he screamed as only a mad Norseman can do, and headed straight for Malroc, intent on decapitating him. Hearing Thain's yell, Malroc turned and sent the fire at Thain and his pathetic band; how dare they attack him. The force of his power hit them and knocked them to their knees, but they did not burn. Brandon was the first to let fly an arrow which, with a wave of his staff, Malroc deflected harmlessly away.

Thadon yelled "Spread out and keep shooting." Rising to his feet Thadon felt dizzy from the effort. Again Malroc waved his arms and sent his power at them and again they all fell but did not burn. More arrows were unleashed but he waved them away. Suddenly, out of the dark, a man charged Malroc from behind, tackling him, sending them both tumbling on the cobblestone roadway. Malroc recovered, sent a power spell at his attacker, freeing himself. Regaining his feet, he had to dodge and roll to his left as he felt more arrows coming his way. With all of his powers, he was still human, and was not fast enough to evade the onslaught of arrows. The stranger's blind side tackle had given Shane enough time to let fly another arrow, which hit Malroc in the left hip, sending a wave of pain through his body as it hit bone. This gave Thain his chance, and he ran at the now stumbling Druid, slashing with his long sword trying to decapitate him. Malroc ducked, and struck back with all his power. Thain screamed, collapsed into a ball, and fell to the cobblestones. Sensing his chance, Thadon sent the fire and Malroc screamed and fell backwards. His wards kept him from burning, and he sent a spell of smoke invisibility towards the attackers. Again the arrows came and two more hit him. In a rage of disgust he threw more smoke at them. Thadon dropped to his knees as did the others and again he sent the fire. The smoke was so thick he could not see Malroc. More arrows were unleashed from Brian and Shawn but they d couldn't see him either. Under cover of the thick smoke Malroc backed away, his legs shaking with the pain of the arrows. Moving back between buildings he stumbled towards his horse. Shoving the arrows thru his legs he broke the arrowheads off. Charring the two ends with fire he forced them back through to stop the bleeding. The one in his hip was worse. He pushed it through and nearly fainted from the effort. Breaking the arrowhead off, he charred the end with an intense heat, then shoved it back in to cauterize the wound inside. The effort made him weak, and beads of sweat broke out on his forehead. How had they done this? His mind rambled from the pain and frustration. Shaking his head to clear his mind, he crawled to an outbuilding. Moving behind it he sent more smoke; then crawled under a side porch. He had to get away before the smoke cleared but could not rise to his feet.

Recovering from the force of Malroc's spells, Thadon managed to reach Thain and rolled him over. Thain moaned and tried to speak but could not. Reaching into his robe Thadon dug out the half empty bag of powder and sprinkled some over Thain, hoping that it might help him recover. The powder sizzled and sparks flew into the air as the powder met Thain's injuries and the spell Malroc had sent into him. He could hear more townsfolk calling out to each other but could not see them.

He heard a woman wail, "Help me, my husband is injured."

"Brandon, do you see him? Does anyone see him? Brian, help me with Thain; I cannot leave him. Shawn get me some water, I need some water. He is burning up inside." Taking the flask from Shawn he lifted it to Thain's lips, who gulped a few swallows down. Pouring the rest over Thain's head and cradling him in his arms he rocked back and forth, holding him tight. Frantic as to what to do next to save him, Thadon gasped, "More water, I need more water." Shane and Brian handed Thadon their flasks, and again Thain took a few gulps. This time he was able to reach for the flasks, and taking one he shakily drank until it was empty, then he let out a sigh and reached for the other one. Thadon helped him, and water spilled down his chin, soaking his heaving chest.

Straightening out his legs he moaned, "Is he dead?"

"We don't know, the smoke is so thick we can't see him." Raising Thain up, Thadon carried him to a nearby cottage.

Collapsing back into Thadon's arms, Thain breathed deeply, "I hurt all over. It feels like a bunch of bee stings."

"You are lucky to be alive. Rest and drink more water. We hit him with the arrows. I saw two of them hit him. He must be hurt but we can't see in this smoke. The wails from the woman cradling her man continued from somewhere in the dense smoke. "Brian, watch over Thain while the rest of us hunt for Malroc, he can't be far." Motioning for the others to follow, Thadon moved warily towards where Malroc had been. Finding the woman holding her man, Thadon knelt beside them. "Did you see where the fire starter went?"

"No, no, I don't care; help me, he's burning up with fever." Taking the bag out of his robe he sprinkled some over the man and moved back as sparks flew and smoke sizzled from his clothes. "Pour water over him and give him all the water he can drink." Signaling to the others Thadon rose, and in a crouch, moved with caution to the other side of the roadway. Kneeling down he whispered to the others, "I can't see anything in this smoke. It's hard to breathe. Let us wait here till it clears."

Brandon touched him on the arm, "my arrow hit him and I saw two more sticking from him. If we crawl on our bellies we can see better, and the smoke is less. We can find him. He can't be far."

Laying down flat on his belly Thadon could see across the road. "Let us move quiet as mice. If you see him, shoot as fast as you can, and I will send more fire." They crawled to the back of the buildings and an alleyway. After a half hour the smoke cleared some and they could stand up. Not finding any trace of him they returned to Brian and Thain.

"We must get back to the River to see what the Romans are doing. They have seen the fires and may yet attack us. Brandon, help me with Thain."

Brandon came over and slipped an arm around Thain's waist, who groaned from the effort. "The man who saved us by tackling Malroc is dead. His woman told me that he attacked him because Malroc set their cottage on fire."

"See to her needs. Her man is a hero. We must help them, but we must get back to the river to see if the Romans are crossing. With Brandon's help, Thadon managed to get Thain moving. Looking around at the still burning buildings and the townsfolk fighting the flames, Thadon took a deep breath and hurried away toward the River and his men.

They hadn't gone far when Thain drew up and pointed at a black horse with its reins hanging down, "That's Balfour's mare." Crossing the roadway they took hold of her reins and examined her.

Thadon calmed the mare, "Shane, Shawn, look for him; he must be near. Malroc may have gotten to him. Brandon, help me get Thain in the saddle, and I will take him to Thelda's. He can rest there. Meet us at the O'Caollaidhe Tavern."

With the cool crisp red dawn, the Romans amassed along the north bank of the Liffey. Thadon called out to the Romans. "Men of Rome, we have stolen your boats. Malroc is defeated. Do not attack us, and we will trade you your boats for the gold you have brought. Leave our land. We have nothing that you need. Malroc lied to you." Backing up, he watched as the Romans stopped their advance. Looking left and right he was pleased that the south banks were full of his men. That should give them pause and delay their attack until Dante could arrive. Turning to Brandon he motioned for him to follow. Calling out to Shane he said, "Sound the Rams Horn if they try to cross. We'll be back soon." Mounting their horses, they wound between buildings, searching for signs of Balfour. They rounded the corner and stopped in front of the Smithy. "I need to find Balfour if he is alive. Now that it is light, let us search for him. He knows where the Druid Book is, and now that Malroc is wounded I need to find it. The skies were darkening and a storm was brewing as they searched behind the buildings and alleyways.

Dante watched as the fog came in, surrounding them in a heavy mist, "Strongarm, call out to the other boats to stay close. Tell them to pass the word. Taking out his compass he watched as it settled down and pointed north. They were rowing south southwest and if they stayed on this heading they would soon arrive at the bay formed by the Liffey River outlet. If they were to help Thadon they had to keep rowing. The winds picked up as the rain set in, clearing some of the fog.

Bracing against the wind Strongarm approached Dante, "The men are fearful for their lives. They cannot see the shoreline. The other ships are falling behind."

"Aye, tis a fearful storm," agreed Dante, "tell the rowers to slow, and we will tie the boats together end to end. Sound the ram's horn, signal them to come alongside."

Torrents of wind driven rain were now falling as Thain watched the Romans moving back from the river bank to the few dwellings and barns on the north side of the river. Still sore from the battle with Malroc, he moved farther under the back porch of the tavern to avoid the wet gusts. Pitching a sack of gold coins onto the table he ordered more whiskey for the men. "Thelda, see that all the men are served. Send the girls out to serve them. The Romans are moving back from the river. This storm has given them pause. Mayhap we will live to fight another day. Craig, keep watch, as I need a rest." Thelda brought him a jug of her best brew. Taking a long swallow he passed it to Craig, who gladly accepted it. His head and shoulder were still throbbing from his wounds.

Thelda watched him closely as he had trouble balancing the jug with one hand. "Your bandages need changing. Save some of that and I'll wash out your wounds with it. 'Tis a good thing the rain has set in, neither of you are fit for battle."

"Aye, but if you sit in my lap and warm me I'll heal much faster," grinned Craig as Thain sat down next to him across from the fire place.

"Look at thee, thou art all busted up, and all thee can think about is what's under a woman's skirt."

Reaching for the jug Thain managed a smile, "Tis true Thelda. When a man might die today and then doesn't , 'tis only natural for him to want a woman, for it may be the last time he can enjoy such a pleasure as only you can provide."

"Aye; 'tis our stock in trade, now hold these bandages while I unwrap Craig's wounds. I need thee healthy in case the Romans change their minds and attack us."

Moving from cottage to cottage, hunched against the rain, Thadon and Brandon made their way towards the north side, looking down each alley as they went. Brandon grabbed his arm and pointed to a pair of legs protruding from a side porch.

Glancing up at the sky Thadon nodded, "That could be him. Help me get his body on the porch. Raindrops dripped off their noses as they rolled the body over. "Balfour, poor Balfour, Malroc smashed his head. His body is stiff. Mayhap he was on his way to warn us of Malroc being here. He was just a kid. Let us leave him here until we can give him a warrior's burial. I need to get to those ruins and recover the Druid's book." After closing Balfour's still open eyes, they pulled their woolen hooded cloaks tight to avoid the wind. Mounting their waiting horses, they guided them around the few remaining buildings, and set out on the ride to the Ruins. The rain and wind slacked as the two riders approached the ruins. Leaving their horses under a lean- to shed, they made their way through the old stone walled courtyard. Thadon caught Brandon by the sleeve and pointed over the wall. They could see a man hobbling out of the old Tower. Cutting across the yard they jumped the short wall and followed the slow moving man. "Hold there, old man, I wish to have a word with you," said Thadon. Startled, the old man dropped what he was carrying and tried to get to his horse and buggy. In a sprint they caught him.

"Please don't hurt me. I'm just gathering my goods. These are my things not his."

Thadon spun him around, "if you mean Malroc, you needn't worry. He's wounded and in hiding."

"Wounded, are you sure? No one can hurt a Sorcerer. He's too powerful."

"I am Thadon, and what I tell you is true. We shot him full of arrows, but he managed to escape in a smoke he sent at us. We mean you no harm. This is my cousin Brandon. We just want to ask you a few questions."

"I recognize thee now. Thou art Eric's son. I used to work for your father in his kitchens. I remember thee; my name is Johnathon."

Looking at the bandages on the old man's head Thadon raised his left eyebrow and nodded to Brandon, "Yes, I remember you. What happened to you?"

"I am poor and Malroc gave me gold if I would cook and clean for him. He was in a rage because you and Thain weren't fighting as he had planned. Balfour was there, he can tell you. When I served him his wine, bread and cheese and Balfour told him you and Thain weren't fighting yet, he flew into a rage and said the wine was no good. He raised his hand and sent fire at me and burned me. He left and hasn't returned, so I was getting my things and leaving when you came. I was leaving him. No gold is worth being burned for. Can I have my things and be on my way?"

"Yes, you can have whatever you can carry from here except his books and potions. I have come to retrieve them. Did you ever see him reading from an old leather bound book?"

"Aye, The Tome he called it. But it's not here. Balfour came and stole it after Malroc left. I saw him. He broke the hinges on the lock to the tower door. I watched him come out carrying it wrapped in a blanket. Sparks flew when he broke the lock. Malroc had put a spell on it but Balfour sprinkled some powder on it and sparks lit up the night. He left on foot and headed north towards the rock hills. I have not seen him since then."

"Balfour is dead. We found his body in town. Malroc caught him before he could get to us."

Brandon caught his arm. "The horn, 'tis the horn I hear. The Romans must be moving again."

Looking off towards town Thadon's ears caught the unmistakable sound of the ram's horn. "Johnathon, we must leave." Reaching into his cloak he brought out several coins. "Will you work for me? Find the book, and I will give you more gold. If you find it keep it wrapped and bring it to me at the O'Caollaidhe Tavern. We go now to fight the Romans. Watch out for Malroc; he is injured but can still cause harm. Will you do these things?"

"Aye, 'tis a shame Balfour is dead. I liked him. I will do as thou wish. You have given me good news. I will search as you say."

"I will return as soon as I can. Search for the book. Balfour may have hidden it." Bidding goodbye Thadon and Brandon returned to their horses and galloped to town. Rounding a corner they came upon Brian riding hard towards them.

"The Romans are moving to the docks. What should we do?"

"Have they crossed the River?"

"Nay, they are staying on the north side."

"Have they attacked you?"

"Nay, nay but they are moving towards the sea. Should we stop them?"

"You ride to the Wood Quay and watch from there. We will ride to the docks and see what they are doing." Kicking their horses into a fast run they galloped through town waving for the men to follow as they past them. Even before they got to the docks they could see boats full of soldiers coming across the river. "Gather the archers. We must stop them if we can." Grabbing the ram's horn Thadon blew three short blasts. "Spread the word. Get the men here as fast as you can."

Brian turned his horse and galloped back towards the O'Caollaidhe Tavern and the men at the Wood Quay. Thain and Craig were just emerging. "The Romans are crossing the river at the docks. Thadon is there, we must help him. Gather your men and meet us as soon as you can." Kicking his horse and yelling at all the men who were now coming out of the many buildings, "to arms, to arms the Romans are coming." He continued through town yelling and screaming at the men to grab their weapons and head for the docks.

Malroc crawled from under the porch he had hidden under. The effort was excruciating. Thadon and his men had almost found him. Thinking quickly he had sent a diversion into their minds and they had turned to search another building. Malroc used the Druid potions in his robe to heal his inner wounds. Moving now, he was more determined than ever to make those pay for this outrage. How had they survived his fire when no one else had? It must be Calcullen's doing. Thadon had used the Druid fire, weak, but it had caught him unprepared and he fumed at the thought of an apprentice besting him. His hatred for his old enemy gave him the strength that he needed to bear the pain in his hip and side. Leaning on his staff he no longer had to act as a cripple; he was one. Every step sent burning pain. Avoiding people, he kept to the alleys and after what seemed an eternity he found his horse. He nearly passed out from the effort to mount the skittish animal. Sending a soothing message into the horses mind he had finally calmed him and pulled himself up using his good leg. His mind swam with thoughts of where he could hide till his wounds healed, but first he must retrieve the Tome and his potions. It had spells he could use to heal his body. Weaving his way through the twisting alleys, he waited behind the last of the buildings before emerging. Watching the road to the Old Monks Ruin before he emerged from behind the buildings, he saw three horses riding fast towards town. Waiting till they were close he sent a mind probe at the leader which diverted them away from him down a different road. Concentrating on his desire to obtain the Magic Compass and his need for revenge he nudged his horse forward and soon arrived at the gate to the Ruin. Hobbling on his staff he was taken aback when he saw the broken lock on the door to the tower. The spell should have prevented someone from opening it. Once more, his sense told him it was more of Calcullen's doings. He cussed him as he made his way inside. Reaching the stairs to the tower he hesitated. Climbing the stairs would be painful and he knew he would not find the book. Turning to the closet under the stairs he opened the creaking door and retrieved his bag of potions and another woolen cloak. His was soaked in blood. Donning the dusty but dry cloak he downed several mouthfuls of a pain reliever potion. He felt the warmth swell inside as the liquids slid down his throat. The Tome was gone. He knew that without going upstairs. It had taken him years to obtain it. Accepting this loss he threw the empty clay jug against the stone wall. His storehouse of bags here would have to do. He could rewrite most of the Tome. Seething inside at the loss of the many spells he had not mastered would not help him now, so he sealed his mind against it. Now he must escape to a retreat where he could heal. Having lived long he had suffered many defeats. Survival was what he was good at and cutting his losses and accepting this setback was just another day in his long life. Revenge would be his in the long run. Reaching down he loosened a floor board and removed his stash of gold. Grabbing all of the bags he could carry he hobbled back to his horse. The liquid potion had numbed him, and after securing his bags he easily mounted. Astride his mount he turned and cast several spells with wards to trap any who would come looking for him. With a look back, he again raised his hands and sent fire at the remaining wood in the Ruin and it burst into flames, lighting the evening with a warm glow. He smiled to himself as he rode away. His plan to destroy the harmony here would work anyway. The Romans would not quit till they acquired the Magic Compass. So be it. Let them destroy each other. He would return after he healed and start his devilment all over again. The thought gave him pleasure and he settled in for the ride. A master potioneer, such as he, would live to fight another day.

    Thadon cursed himself for leaving and searching for the Tome. Rallying his men to fire arrows as fast as they could at the boatloads of soldiers now coming across, he knew the few men who were there with him would not be enough to stem the tide. Heeding Dante's warnings he ordered the few men with him to move back in the middle forming a "u" shaped line of men firing arrows at the shield wielding Romans. The Romans took the bait. Slowly, hiding under their shields, they advanced from the river bank. The ruse was working as the defenders were firing from the sides as well as the front and more Romans were going down. The Roman leader, seeing his mistake, stopped advancing and directed his bowman to fire at the sides while protecting themselves from the front. More and more of the defenders were going down when Thain and a large group on horseback arrived and rode directly at the wedge of Romans hiding behind their bronze shields. Thadon could only watch as

Thain and his men rode into the wedge of soldiers. The horses stomped men and the formation broke into a scattering of men trying to avoid the sword wielding horsemen. Seeing the confusion, Brandon and Brian and the men with them rushed in to meet the now separated invaders one on one. Thadon jumped up and screamed, "Follow me!" Rushing in with the rage of a Demon, Thadon slashed his way to Thain, whose horse had reared from a sword swipe to his foreleg. Reaching Thain he helped him to his feet then backed out of the fray, swinging his sword as he moved back to higher ground. Calling to his men, Thadon sounded the rams horn to retreat," to me, to me; retreat; fallback, retreat, retreat. Brian, take Thain someplace safe, he is wounded." Thain moaned and his head fell forward on Thadon's shoulder. Blood ran down the side of his face as Thadon delivered him to Brian. Thadon kept up the chant, "Retreat, fallback, to me, to me." Gathering the men around him they steadily fell back. The Romans, seeing their chance to regroup, held the ground they were on and did not advance, being contented that they had gained the south bank and could bring the rest of their troops across the river. "Gather the wounded and move back to the high bank. Let the archers volley from there. We will hold the high ground." Shane arrived with a large group of archers. Moving back to the high ground and the west side of town Thadon suddenly stopped and held up his hand, "Listen, 'tis the sound of the drum. Dante is coming; spread out and keep firing arrows. We need to hold them till Dante and the others arrive."

Suddenly Shawn and a dozen men on horseback burst forth between buildings and spurred their horses toward Thadon. "More Romans are coming behind us. They split up. We stayed behind to watch the river as Brandon said. They fooled us. We thought they had all moved to the docks but they didn't. A large group is headed this way. We'll be caught in between." Looking past Shawn in the direction he had come then back to the men they had been fighting Thadon pointed southeast toward the sea.

"We must join with Dante; follow me." Moving to where Thain was lying he lifted him onto his horse and then waved for the others to follow. Darting between buildings, they made a full retreat towards the sea.

Dante watched as Thadon and his men burst forth from the outskirts of Town and headed his way. Reining his horse up next to Dante, Thadon jumped down then helped Thain to the ground. "We wounded Malroc but the Romans attacked this morning."

"Malroc is wounded. Are you sure?"

"Aye, we kept shooting arrows as you said. At least three hit him. Thain attacked him but Malroc cast a spell and Thain fell. I was close, so I sent the fire. He didn't burn but it slowed him and then a dense smoke appeared and we could see him no more. We searched for him but he disappeared. Afterward Brandon and I went to the old Monk's Ruin in search of the Tome. We met an old man named Johnathon. He told us he saw Balfour break the lock on the tower door while Malroc was away and leave with the book wrapped in a blanket. We found poor Balfour dead in town. Malroc must have gotten to him. We don't know if Malroc has the book or Balfour hid it. We heard the horn and returned to town. The Romans were moving to the docks. They had gathered up all the small fishing boats and were crossing the river. We tried to stop them and killed and wounded many, but still they came on. While we were fighting these men, some had stayed back and crossed the river at the Wood Quay to attack us from two sides. When I heard this and the sound of your drums we retreated so as not to be fighting on two sides. I am glad to see you. Did you capture their boats?"

"Aye, we have them. We need to split our men. The Romans don't know we are here. Take your men and move to those hills on the left. We will wait hidden behind this ridge until they attack you. We will come in behind them. Go quickly. Leave Thain with us and I will have Creidon look after him." Dante turned around and signaled for his men to hide, then he moved to the large rock outcropping. Climbing to the top he settled in to watch for signs of the advancing army. Malroc was wounded. Three arrows hit him. Where was he now? Would he leave the area to heal himself? Thinking of what he would do, he realized that Malroc would try and retrieve his bag of potions and the Tome. He should leave now and try to intercept him before he got away. The thought of all his adopted Irish and Norse countrymen dying in this battle solidified his mind into a plan. He must first limit the dying and suffering in both armies. The Romans were following their commander's orders. They would flee if he could get close enough to their leaders and strike at them first. Gazing out across the lush green countryside, he could see an Irish dry stack stone wall running at an angle across the fields towards Town. The wall followed the lay of the land and if he left now he might be at the edge of town before the Romans burst forth. He could use the wall to hide behind, and no one would pay attention to one man anyway. They would be looking for Thadon's army not one man. It was the best way to protect his Magic Compass from falling into the hands of the Romans and save many men in the process. Climbing back down he motioned for Creidon to come to him, "I leave to intercept this army and attack their leaders. I can use the pasture stone wall to skirt the field and circle around them. Watch and wait till the Romans are attacking Thadon before you come out. Tell the men to scream and rush wildly at the rear of the Romans. I will take out their leaders, and with you rushing at them from behind, they will break apart and hopefully flee. Chase them back to the Liffey and beyond. They will go back the way they came from. I go now. May the luck of the Irish be with you, and we will dance in Town tonight."

The Romans arose like a wave over the low ridge on the west side of Town. Standing side by side the sight was impressive. In unison they turned towards Thadon's rag- tagle men, awaiting them on the north flank of a low east west ridge. Behind this line of soldiers rode the commanders, confident that they were about to rout this bunch of farmers and townsfolk with their homemade bows and pitchforks. Thadon passed the word among his men to hold their ground and draw the Romans further from town.

Dante, bent low, continued along the wall and soon found himself behind the turning Roman line. As he suspected, their commanders were well behind and seemed content to watch from a safe distance. Climbing the wall, Dante moved toward the rear of the unsuspecting Commanders. Close enough now, he sent a wave of mind control which kept them focused on the scene before them. Crouching low behind a rock outcrop he focused on the air around the men and began to densify it. Soon a cloud of dense unbreathable air formed around them and they fell clutching their throats, dying as they fell. Rising up and walking to the horses tied to some saplings he mounted a tall bay and gathered up the reins of the six remaining horses. Riding hard towards the rear of the advancing line he screamed at them, then turned and headed to his men now rising in a rush across the low ridge, screaming as they ran, weapons waving in the air. Pulling up as he crossed their line, Dante turned his horse to see the battle field erupt in chaos. No longer in a solid line, the Romans, seeing their commanders dead and the trap unfolding, broke and ran back the way they had come. The moment had come for Thadon to strike, "Archers, fire now!" He watched as arrows found their targets in the backs of the fleeing Romans. Leading the charge, Thadon screamed, "For Ireland." As he rode he heard the same shout ring out, "For Ireland, for Ireland."

Dante, on the stolen Bay, intercepted Thadon as the two groups came together. "Come, we go to find Malroc. Let the men chase them. He will seek out his potions and the Tome. We may yet find him at the Old Monks Ruin. It is our chance to be rid of him forever." Nudging their horses they turned north, galloping across the lush green fields. Thadon's heart raced as fast as his horse at the thought of catching Malroc. With their robes flapping in the wind they skirted the west side of town then hit the road to the Ruin. Up ahead they could see smoke rising from Malroc's lair. Looking around they saw no one about. The smoking Ruin was eerily quiet as they reined in their mounts and tied them to the old stone wall. Jumping the crumbling wall, they made their way towards the still standing stone tower.

Johnathon watched the two riders from his hiding place behind the crumbling stone stables. Recognizing Thadon he called out, "Thadon, hold up, I have news." Turning in the direction of the voice they saw Johnathon coming from the old stable area. The old man smiled as he approached them, "He's gone. I hid when I saw him riding in. Hurt he was, but I didn't dare show myself."

"Dante, this is Johnathon."

"Ah, yes, I remember you, Johnathon", smiled Dante. "Tell me all you can. I need to know which way he went."

"I watched him gather some of his things from under the staircase. He did not go up in the tower. I think he put a spell on this place. You must be careful. He rode north. I was glad to see him go. Before he left he raised his hands and I heard him chanting, then he sent the fire."

"Thank you for the warning. Thadon tells me that you saw Balfour leave with the Tome. Did he have it when he rode into Town?"

"Nay, nay, I would have seen it on the back of his horse. He must have hidden it."

"We asked him to stay hidden and watch for Malroc to move. Do you know where he was hiding? He might have left it there."

"He walked north to those rock ledges." Pointing with his one good arm Johnathon showed them the area Balfour was hiding in. "There are many rock ledges where he could have buried it."

"You have done well, Johnathon," said Thadon." The Romans are scattered and are no longer a threat. If you wish you can stay at the Castle tonight. Dante and I will search for the Tome."

"Yes, let us leave. It is not safe here. I can sense his wards on the Tower. They will wear off in time. The Tome is more important than his potions." Dante clapped Johnathon on the back as the three of them left the smoking ruin. "We will see you at the Castle. Find all the food you can and prepare us a fine meal. We will meet you there." Riding up the hill to the ledges they dismounted. Dante put a hand on Thadon's shoulder. "The Tome has many magic's. Stand still while I extend my mind and search of the presence of magic." Facing the ledges, Dante slowly scanned left then right. Pointing to the right he beckoned Thadon to follow. "It is close. I can smell the powder I gave Balfour to sprinkle on it before he picked it up." Negotiating between the rocks, they soon came upon a cleft large enough to crawl back into. Dropping to their knees they moved into the dark interior feeling with their hands. "These stones, it is under these stones!" exclaimed Dante. Casting them aside, he pulled the blanket wrapped book out of the shallow pit Balfour had excavated for it. "We have it. Let us ride. We must find out how the others are doing. I have long awaited the return of our Book of Spells. This is a great day for our order." Returning to their horses they rode like the wind to the castle. Arriving at the front gates, they were met with men in a jubilant mood. Creidon called out from a stone balcony overlooking the gates.

"Our men are still chasing the remaining Romans. I brought Thain home. He is in his room. He could use your help. His wounds are severe and I fear for his life. He has lost a lot of blood." Carrying the Tome and his bag of herbs from the boat, Dante hurried to Thain's bedchamber with Thadon not far behind.

An hour later Dante sighed, "It is all I can do. The rest is up to him." Looking at Creidon, Dante beckoned him over to Thain's bed. "Call a handmaiden and tell her to watch over him all night and give him water and this potion as often as he can take it." Motioning for Thadon to follow, Dante handed him the Tome, "Let us hide this somewhere where only you and I know where it is."

"I know the perfect place." Leading Dante to his father's bedchamber he lifted a stone in the floor next to the fireplace and deposited the book underneath. Nodding his approval Dante guided Thadon out into the sunshine.

"I look forward to many evenings studying with you while we build those boats to take us to Newfoundland. I will teach you how to make a new Compass. We will need one or two for each ship. By next summer we should be ready to sail. Let us get our families here and have one of your Mother's great feasts. It is a time to celebrate. I studied the writings on Emolac's map. He tells of a noble race of men who live in a virgin land among tall trees. The sun is their father, the earth their mother and the stars guide them. There seems to be no greed or sin against women as in this Judeo Christian Doctrine. Honor and dignity are above all things. They believe in a great spirit that watches over all living things. In their world all life is connected in a never ending circle. Today we have triumphed over those who would use our compass to find land and ruin it. I thank you for helping me keep it a secret. We must not let it slip into their hands. I look forward to living with these people and sharing my life with them."

Thadon stopped walking and turned to Dante. "I also wish to live in a land such as Emolac has written of. After our great feast of celebration I will use the Roman gold to hire the best shipwrights and carpenters. They will build us the boats we need to make the journey. I go now to tell Mother and Shannon that it is safe to join us. When I return I wish to study the Tome and carry that knowledge with me to this new land."

"Tomorrow morning let us ride together. I will go on to Ossury and bring Sonia and Merlin home." The setting sun reflected out across the ocean as they walked to their horses and headed to the O'Caollaidhe Tavern to join their fellows in a round of beer and good cheer.

LaVergne, TN USA
19 January 2010
170410LV00003B/7/P

9 781449 046743